Family
Skeletons

Family
Skeletons

•

A NOVEL BY

RETT MACPHERSON

ST. MARTIN'S PRESS
NEW YORK

PUBLISHED BY THOMAS DUNNE BOOKS
An imprint of St. Martin's Press

Design by Ellen R. Sasahara

Library of Congress Cataloging-in-Publication Data

MacPherson, Rett.
    Family skeletons / by Rett MacPherson. —1st ed.
    p.   cm.
    "A Thomas Dunne book."
    ISBN 0–312–15236–1
    I. Title.
PS3563.A3257F36   1997
813'.54—dc20   96–43048

First edition: March 1997

10 9 8 7 6 5 4 3 2 1

This book is dedicated to my grandmothers,

Kathryn M. Butcher Justice
(1919–   )
and
Launieta Mary Catherine Favier Allen
(1901–1982)

For the sacrifices, the wisdom,
the love.

Acknowledgments

The author wishes to acknowledge the people who
helped bring this book to publication.

Thank you to my agent, Ricia Mainhardt, and my editor, Elisabeth Story, for taking the chance. Thank
you to all the members of my critique group, the Alternate Historians: Tom Drennan, N. L. Drew, Debbie Millitello, Marella Sands, Mark Sumner, and dear, dear
friend Laurell K. Hamilton, who allowed me at least one
nervous breakdown a day. Without them this book would
never have made it out of my computer.

Also, special thanks to fellow St. Louis writers Karyn
Witmer-Gow, Elizabeth Stuart, and Eileen Dreyer for all
of the encouragement to write the blasted thing in the
first place. To my wonderful friend Donna Burgee, who
read it and proclaimed it good.

A special thank you to my mother, Lena Justice
Allen, for . . . all those things mothers do. To my daughters, Rebekah and Elizah, for suffering with me.

And for Robert Michael Yourko, this was too late for
you. Peace.

One

The Lick-a-Pot Candy Shoppe is located on the corner of Jefferson Street and Hermann Avenue, in the town of New Kassel, Missouri. It was at the Lick-a-Pot that I had spent the majority of my morning stirring fudge and listening to Sylvia Pershing give me orders.

My arms were killing me. My shoulders felt as though they belonged to an Olympic athlete. One that had just competed in a decathlon and lost. Stirring fudge is not for the weak of body, or spirit. The smell of chocolate cooking, not to mention the peanut butter, played havoc with my stomach.

I heard an accordion playing in the distance. The jaunty little notes of some polka added the perfect feel to the day's events. Tobias Thorley was our resident accordion player. Even though I could not see him, I knew that he wore his cute little blue knickers that showed off his seventy-year-old legs, and a matching velvet hat with a feather sticking straight out the top of it. He wore the vest over a very blowsy white shirt. This is what he wore every time he played the accordion, and I knew it by heart.

The occasional clink that I heard was from a passerby tossing a coin into his cast-iron kettle, located two feet from him under a nice shade tree.

I am Victory O'Shea, a member of the historical society, of which Sylvia and Wilma Pershing are president and vice president, respectively. I am also the resident genealogist and historian/tour guide. My duties entail just about anything the Pershing sisters can dish out for me to do. Earlier that morning it was turning bratwurst. Now it was stirring fudge.

Dishes clanked across the street at Fräulein Krista's Speisehaus, reminding me just how good her pastries were. The aroma of kettle popcorn wafted in through the oblong windows. I was hungry and sweating profusely, and my husband Rudy and our two daughters were off having fun somewhere. I was stirring fudge.

There was something terribly unjust with this picture.

"Victory O'Shea," Sylvia snapped at me. "I've told you a thousand times that when the shine leaves the fudge it's time to pour it." Her voice cracked with age. It is rumored that the Pershing sisters are well into their nineties, although nobody has ever had the nerve to actually ask them. They wear their silver hair in identical braids twirled on top of their heads, and that is where the similarities end.

Sylvia's eyes are gray and sharp as glass, much like her personality. She is never subtle and doesn't give a hoot if you like her or not. She isn't on this earth for you to like. She is tall and thin, with a bad limp, and has all of her original teeth. The limp was caused by a fall from a horse when she was fifty-seven, and her teeth are healthy because she never eats the fudge that we cook, or any other sweets.

Wilma is soft-spoken and kind, and has peaceful green eyes. She is also shorter and much heavier than Sylvia, basically because she does eat the fudge that we cook, and loves every minute of it. Something Sylvia hates. I don't know if Wilma really likes the fudge all that much, but it is a wonderful way to annoy her sister.

I started to say something hateful in response to Sylvia's order and decided to be respectful, which is what I had done all day anyway.

"Yes, Sylvia," I said instead.

The shop was full of patrons, as it was "Old German Days" in New Kassel. Old German Days is a weeklong celebration that our town has every May. The Lick-a-Pot is owned by Helen

Wickland. Every year she donates the proceeds from Old German Days to the historical society, as do a few other shops. Helen's granddaughter works the counter. She smiles at everybody that comes in, showing off the braces that cost her parents more money than their last car.

"Don't forget," Sylvia said to me. "You've got to give the tour of the Gaheimer House at three-fifteen." It was the fourth time in two hours that she had reminded me, but I said nothing.

I poured the fudge onto the platter that Wilma had buttered for me and smoothed it out with my overly large wooden spoon, wondering what Rudy and the girls were doing in the spring sunshine without me. This was my fifth batch of fudge, and my shoulders swelled from the abuse. A trickle of sweat ran down my temple. Sylvia was on her eighth batch and not complaining in the least. I could not figure out why.

I'm sure it was due to the fact that Sylvia does without caffeine and sweets. Not to mention sex. I suppose I don't want to live to be a healthy ninety-year-old badly enough.

Wilma perked up suddenly and blushed. I knew Rudy must have come in the door behind me. Wilma always blushes whenever Rudy is around. I'm not sure why she reacts that way to him. I suppose a ninety-year-old woman could have a crush on my husband.

I turned to look into chocolate brown eyes that smiled with mischief. Rudy is only five foot ten, but he towers over my five foot two easily. Most people do. He kissed the top of my head and stuck his finger in the fudge for a free taste.

"Hello, Wilma," he said as he winked at her.

"Afternoon Rudy," she said. Her blush deepened. If she blushed any more she'd turn purple.

"What do you want?" Sylvia asked. "Have you come to finally put yourself to good use? Pick up a spoon and spread that fudge before it hardens," she directed.

"Now Sylvia, there's no use in getting all fired up about a bunch of fudge," he said to her, but he picked up a spoon and spread the fudge nonetheless. I felt a sudden surge of pride. Most men wouldn't be caught dead in a candy shop spreading fudge.

3

But my husband bravely faces all of the dangers in life for me.

"Actually," he continued, "I've come to steal Torie from you," he said.

Did I mention he comes to my rescue, too?

"Can't have her," Sylvia snapped. "And her name is Victory. Do you want me to spell it for you?"

Nobody calls me Victory except my mother and Sylvia Pershing. Everybody else calls me Torie.

"Elmer Kolbe said the Gaheimer tour is going to start early. He needs her there."

I studied Rudy's face. He was definitely lying, I could tell. Every time he lies the corners of his mouth twitch. He tried to keep his long face serious. But Wilma stared at him adoringly and Sylvia scowled at him while at the same time, I tried not to laugh. It was a difficult task.

"Well, just who does Elmer Kolbe think he is? I'm the president of the New Kassel Historical Society, not him." She sputtered a few unidentifiable words and added, "Fine, fine. Take her. But you tell Elmer I want a replacement. The historical society depends on the money from this fudge to keep us running all year."

That was a slight exaggeration, and Rudy knew it. But he just smiled and said, "Yes, Sylvia."

"That is Ms. Pershing to you, young man. Don't think because my sister is still ruled by her hormones that you can charm me."

"Sylvia!" Wilma protested.

"It's true. You've never been able to control yourself around men."

Wilma looked truly embarrassed and glanced around the shop to see if anybody had overheard. There were a few customers smiling in our direction as if we were a sideshow. Wilma started to say something, but Sylvia held her hand up and added, "No use in denying it. I remember the fool you made of yourself over John Wakefield."

"That was in 1922!" Wilma defended herself.

"Yes, and that was just the beginning," Sylvia countered.

I pulled off the fudge-covered apron, washed my hands quickly in the back sink, and went out the door. I left the Pershing sisters to debate over something they had debated a thousand times, and Sylvia would win as always.

"Thank you, thank you, thank you, Rudy," I said to him once outside.

"The girls and I thought you might like to eat before your tour."

"Would I ever," I said, and meant it.

"What's it going to be?" he asked.

"How about the Smells Good. A sub sandwich really sounds delicious."

My two daughters, Rachel and Mary, came running across the street. Rudy had dropped them at the Gaheimer House, which is catty-corner to the Lick-a-Pot, with his kid sister Amy.

Rachel is six going on twenty-six, with brown hair and black eyes, and looks extraordinarily like Rudy. Mary is three, and has no desire to be any older. She's having too much fun. She has blondish hair with green eyes and a round face, and looks just like me.

We walked down Jefferson Street, made a right onto New Bavaria Boulevard, and ate a late lunch at the Smells Good.

•

"The Gaheimer House is one of the oldest houses in New Kassel, dating back to the mid-1860s," I said to my flock of tourists. "It is on the register of historical sites in Missouri, along with three of our other buildings. It is now owned by Sylvia and Wilma Pershing, and it houses the historical society's headquarters, and my office."

I love my job. Giving the tours is the only thing that I do in this town that I actually get paid for. I have seven authentically replicated dresses, made just for me to give the tours in. The one I had just changed into to give this tour was an 1870s deep blue polonaise gown, with an open front that revealed an underskirt of the same color. It was trimmed with chenille-ball fringe in a deeper, almost navy blue. I looked like a curtain. The hat

5

matched, and it was just a shame that I wasn't as comfortable as I looked. The crinolette that I wore underneath the dress was stiff and itchy, and the entire ensemble took a good twenty minutes to get on.

"The dress is an authentic reproduction—you may touch it if you like," I said, and held out my arms for the people to touch. For some reason everybody wants to touch a dress that looks like this, so I just let them know up front that it's all right.

We stood in the ballroom, with its marble floor and painted ceiling. My voice echoed off of the walls, and I had to remind myself to speak in a normal tone.

"Before we start the rest of the tour I'd like to ask that you do not touch any of the furniture in the house, as all of the pieces in the Gaheimer House are antiques. Nothing here, except for my dresses, are reproductions. The gentleman behind you is Elmer Kolbe. He is our security. He makes sure that nobody gets lost from the tour."

Elmer smiled at me and rolled his beady gray eyes to the ceiling. He is our fire chief and is supposed to be retiring. He's been saying that for ten years and is still hard at work.

The tour wasn't very large, only about ten people. We moved on to the dining room.

"The paneling that goes halfway up the walls is sycamore. The dining table seats twelve and was brought from Connecticut when Mr. Gaheimer was there on business. Some of the outstanding pieces in this room are the chandelier and the matching gilt convex mirror."

Okay, so it's not the most exciting monologue in the world, but most people at least pay attention. One tourist, though, didn't really seem to be listening to anything I said. She looked at the floor for the most part, wringing her hands, and although it is a beautiful hardwood floor, it couldn't possibly be that interesting.

She was a pretty woman, small and regal-looking. She was one of those women that make men feel big and strong, and other women feel huge, fat, and cumbersome. I felt like a Valkyrie next to her, and I'm only five foot two. She was probably close to fifty years old, judging by the gray hair and laugh lines around her mouth and eyes.

Then it occurred to me that I knew her from somewhere. She owned a shop here in New Kassel. I stopped talking for a while, and she didn't notice. The other patrons looked around the room and at each other wondering if there was something wrong. She still didn't look up from the floor or stop wringing her hands.

I resumed my monologue and went on with the tour. We headed up the steps for the second half and the ninth step creaked, as it always does. I like to think that it is the added weight of my skirts that makes the step creak, and not my weight in general. I am only about ten pounds overweight, but I like to eat, and there is a certain amount of guilt that goes with that.

When I reached the landing I turned around, and instantly noticed that I was missing my hand-wringing tourist/shop owner. I questioned Elmer with my eyes, and he took my meaning and scanned the group, as if I'd just overlooked her.

Why didn't she say something? And where did she go?

When the tour was over, I went downstairs to my office to change back into my street clothes. The next tour wasn't for two hours, and I didn't want to get my dress dirty or wrinkled. Sylvia has them dry-cleaned faithfully every other week, and if there is a mark on them, I am told about it.

There was somebody in my office. I could see the shadow on the wall in the hallway. I expected it to be Rudy or Sylvia, ready to order me to my next duty. Instead, it was the woman from the tour. She stood behind the desk, reading something that lay on top of it.

Caught like a child with her hand in the cookie jar, she flushed, came from behind my desk, and extended a very small, delicate hand.

"Norah Zumwalt," she announced.

I could have sworn that I said something, but I didn't hear it if I did. My expression was enough to warrant her explanation.

7

"I own Norah's Antiques on the north side," she said calmly. "Right off of New Bavaria Boulevard."

"Yes, I know," I said as I shook her hand. Oh, yes, I was thinking, the woman who never has anything to do with any fundraisers or functions of any kind. The woman who closed down her shop during last year's Oktoberfest because the event didn't bring any real customers, just "lookers." Yes, Miss Antisocial Norah Zumwalt. Now I knew who she was.

"What can I do for you?"

"You are the historian here, correct?"

"Yes," I said.

"Have you ever traced a family tree before?" she asked.

"I've done my own and a few others. Why?"

Walking to the only window in the room, she pulled back the lace curtains and looked out at the day's activities. The action could have been done for dramatic effect, but she seemed genuinely apprehensive about telling me what she wanted.

She pressed her palms together, cleared her throat, and turned around to me to begin what seemed like a well-rehearsed speech. "In 1942, my father marched off to war and never came back." Handing me a photograph from her overly stuffed purse, she continued. "His mother was French, I think."

I was still standing in the middle of my office. It's very difficult to sit in the dresses, and since I hadn't had the chance to change clothes, I remained standing.

The man in the photograph was superbly handsome. His hair was wavy black, accompanied by dark, sparkling eyes and a full, pouty lower lip. The overall impression was that of a Mediterranean background.

"Ms. Zumwalt, I don't really have time right now, with the festival and such, to take on any more projects. Besides, this sounds more like a missing-persons type of thing."

"Please. I would like my whole family tree done, but in particular I'd like to find out what happened to my father. I'll pay you as much as you like."

"Well, I normally charge ten dollars an hour plus photocopies, but I still don't know if I'll have the time. The museum is opening this June."

Lord, why can't I just say no to people? I honestly didn't have the time to mess with this. And I wasn't so sure I'd do it even if I had the time. Maybe it was because I'd always thought she was a snob. Whatever the reason, it left me as quickly as it came when I saw her wringing her hands, and I looked down at his photograph again. What must it be like to be fifty years old and not know your father?

"What's his name?" I heard myself ask.

"Eugene Counts," she said as she sat down in a chair next to the wall and smiled.

"When was he born?"

"Probably in 1923."

"Where was he born?"

"Probably in Missouri."

"And his parents?" I asked, expecting her to say, "Probably somebody."

"I don't know."

Well, at least she was certain of her lack of information. After ten years of doing this sort of thing, it still amazes me that people can know so little about their own parents.

"Did he die in the war?" I asked. I tried to take notes by bending over my desk.

"Probably." Back to that again. She looked around the room. It was a tiny room, just off from the ballroom. She stared at the poster, which also served as a map of New Kassel. It read: "Step Back in Time. Discover Historic New Kassel, Missouri, and All It Has to Offer."

"My mother and father never married, and I guess he felt like he didn't have to come home to her when the war was over. He may have found somebody, a woman, in Europe and stayed. All I know is he used to write, then one day he stopped. My mother never asked him about his family."

She pulled out several yellowed pieces of paper from her

9

purse. They were letters, addressed to Viola Pritcher. The lighting in the office wasn't the best, and I had a difficult time reading the faded ink.

"These are two of the last letters that he sent her. I have all the others at home," she said as she arose and went over to the wall opposite the window, where a very old, very pretty rose of Sharon quilt hung on the wall.

The quilt was a donation from an elderly member of the society. The rose parts of the quilt were appliquéd one on top of the other in different shades of pink to give a multidimensional look, and the green vine swirled around connecting the roses. The quilting was very fine, with the stitches accenting the flowers themselves.

"The rose of Sharon quilt was traditionally the bridal quilt," I said to Norah. "Most brides generally had one quilt in that design."

She smiled and hugged herself. "I always want to touch them. Do you?"

"Yes. Quilts have that effect. Go ahead, if you like."

She ran her small fingers across the appliqué roses, lost in her private thoughts.

"So, how far do you want me to go back? How many generations?"

"I don't know. I'd like to know at least who my great-great-grandparents were."

"All right," I said. I reached into the upper left-hand drawer of the Civil War–era desk. It was one of the first items Hermann Gaheimer had acquired for himself when he arrived. "Fill out this form, as best you can. I'll be right back."

I went to the ladies' room. I have no idea why all the women in the nineteenth century didn't die of bladder infections. If I had to live in one of these dresses all the time, I'd limit myself to peeing twice a day.

It took me awhile to get back to the office. I stopped by the soda machine in the hallway and got a Dr Pepper. The soda machine is definitely out of place. It's like a satellite dish in the Amazon forest. Oh well, we must have our caffeine.

When I got back to my office, she was gone. The form, which requested the names, dates, and places of birth and death for the ancestors that she could remember, was barely written on. The photograph and the letters were neatly placed on top of it. Had I really just promised to trace her family tree? Good Lord, it had been at least a year since I had hired out my services.

There was something about Norah Zumwalt and the photograph of her father that rested peculiarly in my consciousness. Now that she was gone, it was as if she had been a mirage or a dream. Why did she follow me through my tour just to ask me this? Why didn't she call me at home or catch me some other time in the office? Why now? Why not five years ago?

TWO

Sunlight filtered through my lavender curtains. It had taken me quite a while to fall asleep the night before because over and over I had read the letters that were written by Norah's father. My eyes were matted shut, my shoulders were sore, and my stomach rumbled.

Our bedroom, along with my office and a bathroom, is located on the second floor of my eighty-five-year-old home. I heard the shower running, and I knew that it was after seven and Rudy was getting ready for work. I got up slowly, wiped the sleep from my eyes, and looked out my window.

The Mississippi River wound in front of my house ever so slowly. A barge crept up the river and the morning sun gleamed off of the ripples it left as it went to its destination somewhere north.

New Kassel is far enough south of St. Louis that we are not bothered by the problems that plague a big city, yet we are still close enough for convenience. My house is on the northeast side of town, away from the shops and tourism, and is perched just right, on a cliff that overlooks Old Man River.

Our property, which is roughly two acres, is bordered by woods on the north side, and Charity Bergermeister's property on the south. River Point Road, and of course the river, are on the east. On the west side of our property, or our backyard, is Mayor Castlereagh's property and home. He owns about eight acres, all fenced, and I can barely see the top of his roof from Rachel's bedroom window.

"Ave Mariiiiia," Rudy sang from the shower. The shower seems to be the only place that he remembers his Catholic upbringing. Unless you want a horror story about one of the saints or martyrs. He is very good at telling stories. He's Irish, and they tell tales with a lot of zeal.

I snuggled back in bed and smelled the Downy on the pillowcases. The girls were up. The aroma of the pancakes that my mother was cooking for them soon smothered out the Downy. I couldn't decide if I wanted to eat or sleep. Finally, my stomach won out, and I headed downstairs.

Rachel was dressed for school. Mary stood on her chair drinking a glass of apple juice. She made gurgling noises in her cup, but stopped after I had given her the evil eye two times.

"Mommy," she said.

"Good morning, girls," I said, and kissed each one of them on the top of the head.

"Mom," Rachel began. She stopped putting "-my" on the end of Mom when she started kindergarten.

"What?"

"Do you know that there are people in this world that don't have arms?"

"Yes," I said.

"That's terrible."

"Yes, it is. Did you discuss this in class or something?" I asked, wondering why she had brought up the subject. Every morning it's something different.

"No. There was a man at the park yesterday that didn't have any arms."

"Oh."

She looked at me wide-eyed, as if I couldn't possibly leave the conversation with just an "Oh."

"That's terrible, honey."

"Mommy," Mary said. "I want a tootie."

"No cookies for breakfast. Finish your pancakes."

I found my mother, who is fifty-two, sitting out on the porch just off from the kitchen. She drank her coffee and watched the river in silence. My parents have been divorced for fifteen years, and after several years of living alone, she moved in with us. She is confined to a wheelchair thanks to polio when she was ten years old. The fact that Rachel has a grandmother in a wheelchair could be why she is always so sensitive to people with other disabilities.

"Morning, Mom. Thanks for getting Rachel ready for school."

"That's okay. I knew you were really tired from all the work you've been doing with the festival."

"Yeah, and I've still got today through Saturday to go."

She seemed to be deep in her own thoughts. I've always thought my mother resembled the Madonna. A Raphaelite version of Madonna, not the version on MTV. She had an oval-shaped face with a small bow mouth and aquiline nose. Her skin was smooth and creamy, and I am completely jealous. Her dark hair was now turning gray and no matter what inner struggle she was dealing with she always seemed calm and in complete control. Just how I would imagine the Virgin Mary. Wonder what Freud would have to say about that?

I left her alone to drink her coffee, grabbed a Dr Pepper, and walked Rachel out to catch the bus. She wore her green-and-red dress with the cows on it. As the bus approached, she looked up at me with serious black eyes and said, "Mom, do you know what the worst part about not having arms is?"

"No, what?"

"All the clothes have sleeves."

In her innocence she couldn't see the much more devastating things in life that a serious disability would cause. To her it was what to do with sleeves. I crouched down next to her and gave her a big hug.

"I think the saddest part would be not being able to hug my children," I said.

Enlightenment dawned on her just as her bus pulled up. I

could see the full implications of what I'd just said play in those dark eyes of hers. She waved then. "Bye, Mom. See you tonight."

I waved and watched the bus until it was completely down the street, then went back inside and headed upstairs to my office. Passing Rudy on the way up, I stopped and gave him a kiss.

I sat down at my desk and dialed the number for the National Personnel Records Center in St. Louis.

"Defense Department," a woman said.

"Howard Braukman, please."

I waited a few minutes for Howard to come on the line. Howard used to be a neighbor when I was a kid in Progress, Missouri. I thought he could save me some footwork on Norah's family tree. While I waited, I took a folder from the middle left-hand drawer and wrote in black magic marker, Counts/Pritcher Client: Norah Zumwalt.

"Braukman," a voice said.

"Howie, are you still trying to sound like a boot camp sergeant? It just doesn't fit you." He was actually sort of cute. It had been at least six months since I'd seen Howie at an anniversary dinner for his parents. Then I saw him again three weeks later, when his mother died. He wore Coke-bottle glasses and had white blond hair. There was something so insecure about him that you couldn't help but befriend him.

"Hi, Torie. How's your mom?"

"Fine." Everybody always asks about my mother first. "Listen, I have a client whose father served in World War II."

"You'll have to have her fill out a form. You know that," he said.

'Yes, I know. The NA13075 and the NA13055. Send them to me, and I'll have her fill them out. But could you do me a big favor?"

"No."

"Come on. You owe me," I said, teasing.

"What do you want?"

"Could you just take a peek and tell me when he died?"

"Absolutely not. Torie, I could get in big trouble."

I waited a few seconds, thinking of what I could do to persuade him. "I could always tell your mother about Henrietta Pierce."

He was silent for a few moments.

"You know I have done lots of favors for you, Howie. Kept lots of secrets."

"This is blackmail."

"I know. Look, I just want to know when he died. The woman doesn't know when her own father died."

"Shit."

"Cuss all you want. But you'll do it? You'll look?"

"It may take me a few days. I do have real work I have to do."

"Thank you," I said. "I suppose I can still keep your secrets quiet." I am just too ornery for my own good.

He didn't say good-bye. He just took down the important information on Eugene Counts and hung up. I really didn't have anything horrible that I was hanging over his head. Henrietta Pierce was his "baby"-sitter when he was younger. I walked in on them once when . . . well, let's just say they gave a whole new meaning to the words "finger painting." Anyway, I would never really tell his mother. Heck, she probably already knew. Mothers have ways of knowing those types of things. And I learned a long time ago that I didn't really have to threaten him to get favors from him. But he liked to create the illusion that he was being coerced into doing me favors.

I glanced down at the photograph of Eugene Counts. From his letters, I did not get the impression that he was the type to forget all about his "dearest Viola" and stay abroad with *ma cherie*. His letters professed his love for her over and over, and that he wished that he could see his hometown of St. Mary's again. I wondered what he was thinking at the time the photo was taken. Too bad the camera couldn't freeze his thoughts as well as his image.

•

It was Thursday before anything earthshaking happened. I was in the office at the Gaheimer House when the phone rang. I had just finished a tour and was still in the vintage clothing.

"New Kassel Historical Society, Victory O'Shea speaking."

"Hi, it's Howie. I mean Howard," he corrected.

"Oh, great. Whatcha got?" I grabbed a pen and tore a piece of paper off of a scratch pad. I suppose I was too excited that he was getting back to me to wonder why he was calling me at my office.

"He's a live one."

"What?" I said. I searched for the chair behind me with my free hand. I found it and sat down, dress and all.

"He didn't die in the service."

"I can't believe it," I said, a rush of excitement bubbling up. I could just see visions of Norah Zumwalt and an ancient Eugene Counts running, arms open to embrace each other, reunited after fifty years. I am such a romantic.

"This is great," I said.

"Yeah. Remember that fire back in seventy-three?" Howie asked.

"Well, I was about ten years old, but I know about it."

"Wiped out over half of our army records up to 1959. But they reconstructed the files for the veterans still alive so they can still get their pensions."

"Terrific. You got an address?" I said, still amazed that the man was alive.

"You said all you wanted to know was if he was dead or alive."

"Jesus, Howie. Have some compassion. I get to tell this woman that her father whom she has never met is alive. But sorry, Howie wouldn't give me an address."

Before I could threaten him with any long-lost secret, his strained voice said, "Eleven-oh-nine West Second Street. Vitzland."

"You gotta be kidding me. That's just down the highway about twenty miles." I wrote it down as quickly as I could. "Anyone else? What's his mother's name?"

"Torie!"

"Last thing."

"Edith."

17

"Thanks. We're even."

"We better be," he said as he hung up the phone.

Wow. He was alive. I had done several lineages before, but this was the first time I really had something exciting to report to a client, something that would make a difference. I dialed Norah's antique shop immediately. No answer. She must have closed down again. I decided I would try her at her home and realized that I didn't have that number with me. I'd call her from my house.

Which I did. No answer there either. Rachel came home, followed by Rudy. I fixed dinner, and we ate. All through dinner I found myself anticipating the moment that I could actually give Norah the good news. Finally, the girls were in bed, and I sat down at the kitchen table to try and call Norah one more time. As I dialed her number, Mom set a spice cake on the table. I immediately devoured a piece.

Mom always has fattening things like that lurking around every nook and cranny. And I feel that I should give them my undivided attention. I consider myself fairly strong willed, but we all have our limits. Some more than others.

The receiver picked up.

"Norah . . . hi. Torie O'Shea."

"Oh, Torie, hello," she said, a little surprised.

My mother came in the kitchen then and gave me a dirty look at the huge chunk that was missing out of the once whole cake. She knew I was the guilty party because I had icing on my upper lip. I tried to lick it off, but I was too late. She laid an open *St. Louis Post Dispatch* on the table and rolled her chair past me to the porch.

"Norah, I've got great news. I'm not anywhere near finished with your family tree. Truth is, I've barely got started. I mean, I've ordered some death certificates, marriage records, you know, standard things. Listen, your father . . . he's alive."

"Yes . . . oh, just a minute. Somebody is at the door." She put the phone down. I heard muffled voices in the background as she answered the door.

Mother came back in the room and frowned even more because this time I had got caught with the cake in front of me. Yes, I was eating another piece of cake as I read the open newspaper. Something caught my eye, and I barely noticed that Norah had come back on the line.

"Can I call you back?" she asked me.

"Well, okay," I said, befuddled. Norah hadn't even given me a chance to say good-bye. That was not exactly the reaction that I had expected. I stared at the phone as if it were the phone's fault.

"Something wrong?" Mom asked me.

Yes. Something was wrong, but I didn't know what.

I studied the words in the newspaper that had caught my attention while I was on the phone. They were circled in red ink, and said: "Wanted: Eugene Counts. Your daughter is trying to find you . . . Norah Z. Reward!!!" The notice was followed by the number assigned to it by the newspaper.

"Hello," Mom said.

"Did you circle this?" I asked.

"Yes. Isn't that the same name on the file you had down here this morning? I remember the name. Wonder why she did that?"

"Did what?"

"Take an ad out in the personals. If she thought he was dead, I mean."

Mother at least had the decency to blush, making her perfect, creamy skin radiate.

"Were you reading my files, Mother?" I asked with a half smile.

"You shouldn't leave them lying around," she said. I thought the same thing about all of her fattening goodies, but she didn't listen to me. "You doing the grocery shopping tomorrow?" she asked me, all innocence.

"You nosy rosie!" I swatted her with the newspaper. "Maybe I will," I said, shoving a big piece of cake in my mouth. She looked appropriately horrified.

"How are your children supposed to learn anything if you show no self-control?" she asked me.

"Why do you make the stuff if you don't want me to eat it?

I mean, you go to all the trouble to bake it, you set it out on your pretty china plates, and then I'm not supposed to touch it? Jeez, that's cruel and inhumane punishment. Even Job couldn't pass on that temptation."

"I don't care if you eat your share. But it would be polite if you didn't eat everybody else's."

I sputtered. She stammered and rolled out of the kitchen, leaving me to contemplate just why Norah would put an ad in the personals if she thought her father was dead. The ad had to have been placed before I found out that he was alive. Had she known he was alive, or was she just taking a stab in the dark?

No matter which way I mulled it in my mind, it still rested uneasy.

Three

Norah had not called me back. Not that night and not the following morning. I waited until after lunch and then called her house. The line was busy. I dialed her antique shop, and after the third ring a very irritated woman answered the phone.

"Betty," was all she said.

"Hello?"

"Norah, is that you?" she asked.

"No. This is Victory O'Shea. I'm looking for Norah. She's not there?"

"Oughta give you a prize," she said.

"Do you know where she is?" I asked.

"No," she said. Her voice was deep and rough, as if she'd smoked three packs of cigarettes a day for twenty years. "She was supposed to be in at one and didn't show. She didn't even bother to call. I'm sitting down here without anyone to help me. And I know I can just kiss a lunch break good-bye."

"When did you talk to her last?"

"I don't know. Are you a customer or a friend of hers?" she asked.

I found that question somewhat frightening. To think this woman had been speaking to me this way and thought I was a customer. I forget there are people like her.

"Friend," I finally answered.

"Well, you tell her I'm ticked. I don't know how to do the cash drop at the end of the night."

"Sure, okay," I said, and hung up the phone.

Call it overreacting, but I was worried. I hopped in my station wagon and headed out Stuckmeyer Road to Wisteria. The town of Wisteria is located southwest of New Kassel, and has a population of about four thousand. Norah had lived there for a number of years.

Before Norah came to the Gaheimer House that day, my only thoughts of her were that she was antisocial. I didn't really concern myself with her all that much. Now, it was amazing all the things that I knew about her. She had two children. She was divorced. I even had her exact address, thanks to the form that she had filled out.

My car moved at a snail's pace, thanks to the road construction. Big yellow vehicles were strewn all over the sides of Stuckmeyer Road. Construction people walked out in front of moving traffic without giving it a second thought. I don't know if they did it because they knew we would stop or because they had become oblivious of the traffic.

A huge man who resembled a grizzly bear stood with a sign that said, Slow. No duh, I thought. He waved my side of the traffic on, while the other side had to stop and wait. They had taken a four-lane road down to two lanes.

I love the sign that talks about Missouri tax dollars at work. I wondered whether, if I suffered a nervous breakdown from their road construction, the tax dollars would pay for my Prozac.

A ten-minute drive took nearly thirty minutes. I had an itch where my collarbone was. I thought it was just irritated from my shirt. Wrong. I took a good look in the mirror and saw that I had broken out in hives. My palms were sweaty, making it impossible to get a good grip on the steering wheel. I hate traffic. I hate waiting. I was really concerned that Norah was very ill or could have had an accident.

I found Norah's street and turned. The street was perfectly quiet, peaceful looking. Manicured lawns bordered the street, with large ranch-style homes placed in perfect symmetry. Large oak and maple trees stood proudly in each yard, shading the majority of the street.

It was the perfect neighborhood, like something out of a movie. House number 2112 looked no different than any of the others. Except that the front door was open. It wasn't gaping open, but it was open. That disturbed me.

I could just see Norah being abducted and carried away. She couldn't possibly put up much of a fight, since she was very small. I stopped in the middle of the street and parked the car. I left my keys in the ignition as the annoying, *ding, ding, ding*, reminded me. I didn't care.

"Norah?" I yelled as I got out of the car. The warm air felt cool against my back where the sweat had pooled. I wore jeans and a pink cotton shirt. I should have worn shorts.

I could see more of the inside of Norah's house the closer I got. I slowly pushed the door the rest of the way open. My voice full of anxiety, I yelled, "Norah?"

There was no answer. The TV was on. Maybe she was just out in the yard and had forgotten to shut the door. And forgotten to put the phone back on the hook. And forgotten to call in sick to work . . .

"Norah? Are you all right?" I was seriously concerned about her at this point. She could be in a coma or she could have fallen down the basement steps. All sorts of things could have happened to her. Then again, she could just be in the shower, having decided to tell the rest of the world to go to hell today. Boy was I going to feel silly when she jumped out of the bathroom in a towel.

Turning down the hallway to the left, I was immediately struck by the pungent, sickly sweet odor. I'd never smelled anything quite like it and probably never will again. Every nerve in my body stood up and saluted.

My hands trembled and my stomach clenched. Funny how every muscle can become like jelly. It wasn't anything physical. It was fear. Fear made my body react in a physical way. I wiped my hands on my blue jeans, noticing how rough the material felt. Were these my old jeans? No, must have been my new ones.

Dear God.

Long before my eyes ever landed on Norah, I knew what had

happened. There was blood on the walls and ceiling. It left an almost artistic splattering, as if in some perverted imitation of a Picasso. There was more blood on the bed, and a huge puddle flowed away from her neck on the floor. An ocean of red spilled farther from her, carrying her life with it.

I couldn't move. Her hand still clutched the telephone receiver. I imagined the horror of her attack. The fear she must have felt. The indescribable pain. And yet, all the while, she had clutched the telephone receiver. Had she used it as a weapon? Or had she been just too frozen in fear to think to drop it?

She was partially on the bed, with her head thrown back toward me, hanging over the edge. The sheets were a red, mushy mess, and a slight squeal escaped my throat. Her eyes bored into me. Lifeless doll's eyes now. Had she watched her murderer leave? Or was she already dead when he left?

Finally, the only movement I could make was the slumping of my body to the floor. I landed on my knees not an inch from the puddle of blood, and expelled what seemed like everything I had eaten in a year. My gut wrenched time and time again.

Oh, Mother of God.

•

I finally made it to my feet and ran from the room, using the hallway walls to keep me standing. Bursting through the front door of Norah's house, I landed in her yard on my knees. All I knew was that I had to get to a telephone. It was that determination that got me up off of my knees and running to the house next door.

I rang the doorbell, then pounded on the door. The curtains moved, but nobody answered the door. I pounded some more, never feeling it. I was numb. I was hysterical.

"Please, God. Open the door. Open the damn door!"

I heard the chain unlatch, and the door opened slightly.

"Nine-one-one. Call nine-one-one!" I yelled.

The phrase "little old lady" was a perfect description of the woman who stood behind the door. Snow white hair was perfectly curled around her face, and sky blue eyes peered from behind metal framed glasses.

"Please, call nine-one-one. It's Norah. She's . . . dead."

Finally, she opened the door and let me in. I felt terribly guilty bringing this to her house on this otherwise beautiful day. She started to shake, and then cry. We were now in hysterics together.

She managed to get up and get me a glass of water while I dialed 911. I then ran to the bathroom and everything that I'd just drunk came up as well.

I ran some water in the bathroom sink and splashed it on my face and over my short hair. The face in the mirror didn't seem to be mine. My skin was normally green. Mother says it's olive. I say it's green, and it looked more so now. Actually, as unjust as it was, I looked just like my father. Put a dress on my dad and that's me. But as I stared into the mirror in this stranger's home, the face looking back at me seemed more the stranger than did the little old lady.

My intestines felt like they were doing the rumba, and I shook from head to toe. Overall, though, I thought I held together fairly well. Then I began to cry uncontrollably. I hadn't even known her. Not really. But the memory of what someone had done to her brought the tears on like a monsoon. I was angry, and what's worse, I felt helpless. Helplessness is not something I like to feel.

I heard the doorbell ring a few minutes later. It was Sheriff Brooke. Just what I needed. Sheriff Brooke and I go back a long way. He arrested me once. Yes, I confess. I have a record. I was speeding through town in my husband's GMC truck, and I argued with the sheriff over the ticket that he tried to give me. Then I resisted arrest. When he realized that I had been trying to get Charity Bergermeister to the hospital before she had her twins, he gave us an escort. Once we were at the hospital, he arrested me.

Anyway, we have never got along since then; we just sort of tolerate each other.

"Hello, Torie."

25

"Sheriff Brooke."

He sat down in the chair opposite me. The furniture looked like something out of 1962, in your average brown. White lace doilies were poised just perfectly over the backs of the chairs and the couch. The little old lady sat perched in her rocking chair, waiting to listen to every word we said.

Brooke was off duty, and so he had no uniform. His eyes were blue, his hair sandy. He looked like a man to be reckoned with, and as much as I hate to admit it, he *was* a man to be reckoned with. His shoulders were very broad for his height. He was wearing jeans and a short-sleeved T-shirt with a camel on it. It was the camel that advertises the Camel cigarettes. The camel wore sunglasses and had a cigarette hanging out of his mouth. Funny how that is what grabbed my attention.

The shirt suited Sheriff Brooke, I decided. I had often wondered if his mother secretly called him "Bubba."

"So, you found the body?" he asked.

"Yes."

"What made you come all the way out here?"

"It's only ten minutes away. It's still in your jurisdiction," I said. "I was worried about her. She didn't show up for work. Or even call in sick." I rubbed my eyes. "She was supposed to call me back last night and didn't. I was worried that she might be seriously ill."

"How well did you know her?"

"Not real well. She was a shop owner. I've talked to her a few times at council meetings. That sort of thing," I answered. I felt like a robot on autopilot. The answers to his questions were just rolling out of my mouth without my giving them much thought.

"So, why would you be so concerned about somebody that you barely know?"

Did he think *I* was a suspect? "She recently came to the Gaheimer House to ask me to trace her family tree. Or at least part of it anyway."

"Did you touch anything?" he asked.

"Just the front door."

"The knob?"

"No, I just pushed it open."

"Notice anything unusual?" he asked.

"Besides the dead body and all of the blood? No, not a thing."

He glared at me as he stuck a piece of gum in his mouth. "You know, I think that every time I have ever spoken with you, you've had tons of attitude. I think that maybe you're too big for your britches."

"Well what kind of question was that?" I said angrily. "What do you mean did I notice anything unusual? I noticed lots and lots of blood, and that's about as unusual as I get to see in a given day."

He must have decided that, considering what I had just seen, I was allowed some attitude, because he didn't say anything back to me.

"Any unusual cars?" he asked finally. "Anything out of place?"

"I told you, I wouldn't know. I didn't know her well enough to know if anything was out of the ordinary."

"Any idea who she was talking to on the phone?"

I swallowed hard and hugged myself. Was it possible that she was still holding the phone from when she had spoken to me last night? "Me," I suggested.

He stopped chewing for a minute and swallowed. It would have come as no surprise to me if he had swallowed his gum.

Deputy Newsome came in the front door then. His face looked as if it belonged to a thirteen-year-old. Pudgy red cheeks showed no trace of any facial hair.

"Hey, Torie," he said to me.

"Hey, Willie."

"My mom really appreciated the lilac cuttings."

"Good. Tell her if she needs some more to let me know."

"Newsome," Sheriff Brooke spat, "did you come in here to talk to Mrs. O'Shea about botany or was there some official matter that you needed to discuss?"

"Oh, yes sir. The victim hasn't been dead long, and—"

"How do you know?" I asked.

Without hesitation he turned to me to elaborate. "The blood is too fresh, hasn't begun to dry or anything. No rigor . . . I overheard the ME—"

"Excuse me!" the sheriff barked. "This is a witness, not a cop."

"Oh, sorry. Sheriff, the ME wants to speak with you. Says the perp could have been here as little as an hour ago."

"Tell me you've got people scanning the subdivision."

"Yeah," he said. "But Ms. Langsdorf here is about the only person home on the whole block."

"Whatever. I don't care if it's a block away. I want everybody questioned."

Brooke held up a finger to tell me to wait a minute, then went outside to speak with the ME. The thoughts of being on the other end of the phone when Norah's assailant arrived really made me sick. Then I remembered Deputy Newsome saying she hadn't been dead very long. That made me even more sick. I could have actually walked in on that!

I could have possibly even saved her if I had gotten there in time.

Brooke came back in the door, pinching the bridge of his nose. He wrote down everything while we talked this time, which made me extremely nervous.

"Why do you think she was on the phone to you when she was killed?" he asked.

"Well, I don't think that anymore."

"Oh, and why not?" he asked. "In five minutes' time you just change your mind?"

"I called her yesterday, Thursday, and she hung up quickly. She said somebody was at her door. I haven't talked to her today. If she died this morning, it couldn't have been me on the phone."

"Do you know who was at the door?"

"I couldn't tell."

"Who do you think killed her?" he asked me.

"I wouldn't have any idea," I said. "I didn't know her well

enough to know who would have motive or anything else," I said.

The sheriff watched me closely over the top of his notepad. "All right," he said. "You can go, for now. I'll have to speak to you again, at a later date."

"Fine," I said as I stood up. "Thank you, Mrs. Langsdorf, for letting me use your bathroom." She only nodded and raised her handkerchief to her nose.

"Be gentle with her," I whispered to Brooke. "She's had quite a scare today."

I left her house, breathing in the fresh air. I headed toward my car, wanting to be home, and having no idea how I would ever make it there.

"Oh, Mrs. O'Shea?" Sheriff Brooke asked as he came out of Mrs. Langsdorf's house.

At that moment I thought I was stuck in a *Columbo* rerun. Why did he have to wait until I got halfway to my car to ask me a question? "What?" I snapped.

"Where's the dog?"

"The dog?" I said, loud enough that he could hear me.

"There is a dog bowl with food and water. No dog."

"How the heck should I know?"

Afterward, he probably thought of me as I had thought of Betty at the antique shop earlier. I didn't really care, though. All I knew was that I wanted out of there, and I was about ready to have a full-blown panic attack.

I sat in my car and laid my head on the steering wheel. I turned the engine over and the radio came on. The weather. It was supposed to rain. I felt oddly detached from the entire world. The radio sounded strange. The steering wheel felt funny. The world went on. How could everything just keep going? A life had just been ended, horribly. I had just seen probably the worst thing I would ever see, and now the radio was advertising two-by-fours just a $1.69 at so-and-so's, for your new deck this summer.

THE NEWS YOU MIGHT MISS
by Eleanore Murdoch

E veryone will be happy to hear that Old German Days was a success! Thanks to all of you that showed your support and volunteered. And of course a special thanks to Torie O'Shea for suffering through a solid week in those hot historical costumes.

Sylvia Pershing reported that a record amount of money was raised by the Lick-a-Pot Candy Shoppe, Quilts and Things, and the Dog and Suds for the historical society. She wouldn't give me an exact amount, but it was somewhere in the neighborhood of $4,600. Great work!

Also, we were all deeply saddened at the death of a fellow shop owner, Norah Zumwalt, who owned Norah's Antiques. Our prayers are with her family.

Tobias Thorley wants to know who stole the statue of Abraham Lincoln out of his garden. If you'll just return it he won't press charges.

And, last but not least, Noble Quimbly puts out a challenge: Anybody that can hit his ex-wife's photograph between her eyes with a dart, he'll buy you a beer. Until next time.

Eleanore

Four

Norah's funeral was three days later. In my life so far, showing up at the funeral home was one of the hardest things that I ever had to do.

She was laid out at Klondike and Sons Funeral Home in west St. Louis County. Norah was the only member of her family that had lived down South. Her three sisters and her children all lived in and around St. Louis.

I was nervous, and Rudy gave my shoulder a squeeze as he opened the funeral-home door for me.

We entered the hall and that familiar funeral-home smell instantly filled my nostrils and set off an alarm in my head that told me to be quiet. Why people are quiet in a funeral home I'll never know. It's sort of like a cemetery. It's not as if the dead will complain, and you'd think the living would welcome the diversion.

The casket was closed, as I thought it would be. I can't remember if any of the knife wounds had touched her face or not.

A man stepped from the casket and the small knot of people that he was speaking to, and came my way. He was extraordinarily good-looking. His stark blue eyes only served to make his face seem more chiseled than it really was. He looked to be about twenty-eight years old, with dark wavy hair. He was Adonis rediscovered.

"Hello. I'm Jeff Zumwalt," he said, extending a hand.

I felt myself stiffen and suck in my breath. This was Norah's son. I didn't know what to say to him. If I mentioned that I was the one that found his mother's body, he might break down. And I didn't think I could handle that. What if he somehow blamed me? That would be even worse. I couldn't speak. I stood there staring into his blue eyes and completely ignoring his outstretched hand.

"Hello," Rudy said, and shook his hand. "I'm Rudy O'Shea and this is my wife, Torie."

Something registered in his eyes. It was just a split second, but it was there.

"You're the one that found her," he said with no particular emotion in his voice. I couldn't tell if he was appalled by that or sad. He could even have been happy for all I could tell.

"How did you know my mother?" he asked.

"I'm the chief historian for the New Kassel Historical Society. Our headquarters are just two blocks away from your mother's shop. She hired me to trace her family tree."

"I see," was all he said.

"I can't tell you how sorry I am," I said. "I thought, I'd go ahead and finish her family tree for you and your sister."

"Rita would love it," he said as he played with the cuffs on his shirt. It was a white cotton oxford type of shirt, worn under a suit jacket. Anyone could buy it at Kmart for twelve dollars. He probably paid fifty bucks for it. He looked the type to deliberately spend too much money for something.

"She is just like Mom was," he said. "Always thought she'd find somebody great back there in her ancestry. A king, a Revolutionary War hero. I think she always wanted to join one of those societies or something. What difference does any of it make? It seems fairly trivial in light of everything that has happened. Don't you agree?"

I was slightly defensive toward his attitude, but I'm always defensive. "I didn't get the impression that she was looking for anybody great or famous. I think she was more concerned about finding something on her father."

Just then an elderly couple came by. The woman touched

Jeff's arm and shook her head. "I'm so sorry, Jeff. She was a sweet woman," she said.

Jeff touched her hand with his and smiled. "Yes, she was. Thanks for coming."

Jeff turned to me then and looked to the ceiling to think of what it was he wanted to say. "What were we discussing? Oh, yes. Her father. She'd been obsessed with that angle for years. Not that I blame her. But I don't see how any of it would make her a better person."

His attitude was not an unusual one. A lot of people could really care less about that sort of thing. Still, it irked me, and I could tell that Rudy had read my thoughts. He leaned closer and put his hand on my shoulder.

"Well," I said to Jeff, "he who knows not where he came from, knows not where he's going." Somebody important said that, but I couldn't for the life of me remember who it was.

He smiled at me. "Rita will greatly appreciate your efforts."

"Where is your sister?" I asked. "I'd like to pay my respects to her before we leave."

"She is not here at the moment. She took her children to get some dinner. She should be back shortly."

"May I have her address?" I asked.

"Of course," he said. "Let me get a piece of paper. I'll be right back."

As he walked away, Rudy turned me around to face him. His brown eyes were serious, like they are when he's getting ready to scold one of the girls. "What are you trying to do?"

"Nothing."

"Well what was all of that 'he who's going doesn't know where he's going' crap?"

"He ticked me off. Don't you think he's got a rather flippant attitude?"

"Did it ever occur to you that maybe he doesn't really give a damn about her ancestors because he's more concerned with her being dead?" Rudy asked. He tried to keep his voice low, but the last two words of the sentence were raised somewhat.

"Well . . . well . . . he shouldn't be rude to me. I was just of-

33

fering to do a service for them—one that their mother wanted me to do—and he just dismisses it like it's the world's most ridiculous thing."

"It probably is to him. Nothing makes any difference to him right now. His mother is dead."

I hung my head. Rudy had made his point. I suppose I was having difficulty being objective.

Jeff came back with a piece of paper that had his sister's name, address, and phone number on it. He handed it to me with a cool smile.

"Thank you," I said. "I'm sorry if I seem a little . . . testy to you. Finding her has affected me very much."

"I understand completely," he said.

"Can I ask you something?" I said to him.

"Sure," he said.

"When did you see your mother last?"

With that question, Rudy kicked the back of my knee and coughed. I gave him the sweetest smile that I have ever given anybody in my life.

"Thursday," Jeff said, without having to think about it.

"Did she act strange? Did she have any prank phone calls, a strange teenager in the neighborhood? Problems at work?"

"The only problem she had at work was the fact that the place existed."

"What do you mean by that?" Rudy asked, before I could.

"She insisted on owning the shop. She didn't need the money. As a matter of fact, she had to use some of her personal money every year just to keep it afloat. It served no purpose whatsoever."

"Why didn't she need the money?" I asked. "If you don't mind my asking," I added. He didn't have to answer me—I was a complete stranger—but he complied.

"She was independently wealthy," he stated without blinking. "But, in answer to your real question, I have no idea who could have killed her. I know that's what you're driving at. I have tried to pretend that there was this horrible man who picked her out, just her, for some special reason."

34

"Why?"

"Because there would be a reason for it. I can't bear to think that what happened to her was random."

Somehow I didn't think there was a reason on earth that would make me feel any better, if it had been my mother. But I understood exactly what he meant.

I thanked him for his sister's address, and turned to leave the room. Rudy walked close to me, hand on my shoulder. As we walked through the glass doors into the lobby, Sheriff Brooke came in from the outdoors.

"Mrs. O'Shea," he said. "Rudy." He was in official uniform today, and he reached up and touched the brim of his hat when he spoke our names.

"Good afternoon, Sheriff," Rudy said.

"Sheriff," I managed. I kept on walking right out to the parking lot, but Rudy stayed behind in the lobby for a few minutes. Their conversation was short, but seemed to be polite.

When Rudy came out to join me, I asked him what they had talked about.

"Hockey," he answered.

Yeah, right.

Five

You're a real bitch lately," Rudy said. His expression was one of concern, not anger, and so I let his remark ride.

It was true, I could keep up with the best of the bitches, if pressed to do so. I was cranky, high tempered, self-absorbed, and moody.

Every now and then these submerged personality flaws of mine will surface, eventually moving on. But I had been this way for days, and had expected Rudy to say something eventually. Bless his pea-pickin' heart, it had taken him three days of being treated like the soles of my shoes before he said anything.

I don't always behave like this. Usually I'm the one trying to figure out what is wrong with Rudy. He is very moody, and can go from a charming Cary Grant to Freddy Krueger in under an hour. It really is quite a remarkable metamorphosis.

He stared at me from across the kitchen, eyes following every move I made. I grabbed a handful of Fritos, the barbecue kind because they make my breath smell so bad that Rudy can't come within arm's distance of me. Shoving them in my mouth, I gave him the look of flying daggers. I think he actually flinched.

"What is it? PMS?" he asked as he leaned up against the counter.

"I don't get PMS." Right. Famous words of every self-righteous woman, trying to keep her dignity. I'd much rather be a bitch for a reason than because of hormones. It seems like such a waste of long-harbored anger, not to mention energy, for it to be used on hormones.

Rudy threw his hands up in surrender and reached into the refrigerator for the milk. Okay, if I didn't concede soon, then he would be in a winner of a mood, and I'd spend the whole night trying to get him out of it.

I wanted him to notice. I wanted him to ask, plead, and pry out what was the matter with me. But there was a fine line to the rules of this game. I had to concede at some point after I'd made him miserable, or then he'd get angry and we'd all suffer. And his moods were a heck of a lot worse than mine.

Funny, this thing called marriage. It reminded me of a ship on the ocean. You just have to ride the waves and hope that you don't slam into any rocks.

Rudy's surrender was the point for me to begin to give a little. I don't think that there is a manual on any of this, but we spent the first four years of our marriage just figuring it all out.

"I'm just tired," I said. It was bull, but it was an opening without revealing too much. He'd bite.

"I think . . ." He tested his ground and, surprisingly, was straightforward. "I think that you are still upset over finding the body," he said as he twisted the cap off of the milk, but made no move to get a glass.

"Body? She had a name. Norah Zumwalt. She was a real person. Besides, wouldn't you still be upset? If it were you who had seen what I saw, you still wouldn't be sleeping."

"Maybe you should see a shrink," he said. He raised the milk jug to his mouth.

"Don't you dare drink that milk without a glass! And my head is shrunk enough."

"Yeah, by self-diagnosis," he said, reaching into the cabinet for a glass.

"No, when I was a kid, a bunch of headhunters broke into my house. They had just begun to shrink my head when my dad jumped in to save me."

Leave it to a six-year-old to walk into a room when you've just said the most stupid thing in your entire life. Her eyes were wide with wonder. "Really, Mom? What did Grandpa do? Beat them up?"

I laughed slightly, tension broken. "I'm just joking, Rachel. Go on and play," I said, patting her on the head.

"If you want to know the truth," I began. "It's damned hard to live with the fact that I might have been able to save her."

"No. You might have been killed, too, and then where would Rachel and Mary be without a mom? It's sad, yeah. But Norah's children are at least grown. It was fate. You were spared."

"Gee, I feel better," I said. "Why did she have to die at all? Why did the whole thing have to happen?"

I couldn't help but feel a cold chill run down my back. Why? That summed up my problem. It was senseless. It didn't look as though she'd been raped. From what I could remember, her clothes were on and in order.

Robbery? Well if it were robbery, why didn't he just slice her throat? According to the papers, she had been stabbed repeatedly. How many robbers would have wasted all of that time stabbing her? The entire situation lacked a motive.

I thought of Jeff Zumwalt's words about it being random. Yes, I agreed with him. If it were random, that was the most unsettling notion of all. Because then, nobody would be safe from it ever happening to them.

Rudy gulped his milk and then walked across the room toward me. He hugged me and gave me a kiss, Frito breath and all. For the moment I felt a little better.

•

I sat in a booth at the closest Pasta Club, waiting for Rita Zumwalt Schmidt. I had phoned her to see if she would meet me for lunch, and she had agreed.

The Pasta Club is in south St. Louis County. It had taken me an hour to get there, but their food is well worth the drive. The waitresses all wear an off-the-shoulder white blouse, with a bodice laced under their breasts, and a skirt. They look like they've been out smashing grapes. The waiters wear a very blousy white shirt, with knickers that tie on the outside of the knee. They resemble gondoliers. You can't get any more Italian than grape stompers and gondoliers.

I knew the instant Rita arrived in the doorway who she was. She was small like her mother, probably thirty or so, and very graceful. She was dressed conservatively, but fashionably. She was one of those women who always look fresh, clean, and in complete control. Her clothes fit perfectly, no puckers, no gaps, no wrinkles. She was wearing a pair of tan dress pants and a tan-colored blouse with green swirls in it, and the proper adornments of jewelry.

Nothing was overdone. Even her makeup appeared very light, but was actually the whole nine yards. Several base coats of the perfect color, blush, three subtle shades of eye shadow, mascara, liner, and lipstick. Amazing. The overall effect was as though she wore nothing at all.

How do women do that? On my best days I wear some mascara, maybe some blush. My hair never looks good, and my clothes are a wreck. I could iron for a year and still have wrinkles. Nothing ever fits right, thanks in part to my short waist.

So I sat across from Miss Perfect, feeling more inadequate by the moment. Her hair was an average brown, eyes an average blue. Her weight was perfect. I hated her from the start.

She'd probably order a salad.

"I'm so glad that you called," she said. Perfect manners, too. "Mother was very excited about the work that you were doing for her."

"Well, thank you for coming," I said.

The waiter appeared, and I hesitated to order. I didn't want to order enough food for the Confederate army if she was going to order a salad. So I waited.

"I am famished today," she said. "I'd like a martini, with a salad," she said. She bit her lip and leaned forward to me. "Would you like to split a pasta order with me?"

I was going to barf. "No thanks," I said. "I'm a pig and I usually eat everything on my plate."

She laughed dutifully, as if it were a joke. Little did she know.

The waiter smiled. He was tan, with white teeth and black hair. I imagined his parents had just come off the boat. I glanced at his name tag and was very disappointed when I saw his name was Scott. I expected Giovanni or something.

"I think," she began, "I will order the manicotti, but please bring me two doggy bags. One for my salad and one for my pasta. I will never eat all of it," she said to the waiter, who just smiled.

He turned to me, waiting.

"I'll have an order of fried zucchini, with a salad and an order of the fettuccine Alfredo. I won't need a doggy bag."

He winked at me. "Anything to drink?"

"Dr Pepper."

The waiter departed, and I stole a quick look at Rita without her knowing. In all fairness, she looked as uncomfortable with me as I was with her.

"I've decided to go ahead and finish your mother's family tree," I said. "It's a gift."

"How nice," she said. "Mother was really hoping to find something on her father's family."

"Yes, I know. He's alive."

Her face was blank. "What?"

"Her father is alive. I haven't contacted him as of yet. I'm not sure how to approach him."

A tear welled up in her eye. "My God. After all these years. I have a grandfather," she said, amazed.

"Yes," I assured her. "I may try and contact an aunt or uncle or old neighbor first and get their reaction. Sometimes people don't appreciate surprises like these, especially at the age of seventy."

"Of course. You'll let me know, won't you?"

"Oh, yes."

Our salads arrived with that wonderful bread I always eat too much of. "I was curious," I said. "Where are your mother's things?"

"The police told me a few days ago that I could go through her things now. Jeff wants very little, just a few photos. John only wants a few sentimental things. Things that they acquired on vacations. That sort of thing. So I've moved her personal things to my house. I haven't moved her furniture or anything."

"I'm sorry, but who is John?" I asked.

The look on her face was worth a thousand dollars. She was upset with herself for letting something slip.

"He's Mother's boyfriend."

"Boyfriend? Oh. Well that's certainly none of my business. I was just slightly confused for a second. I thought maybe John was a son I knew nothing about."

"No, no. They'd been seeing each other for years. It really wasn't all that serious. I just took it as two older people having somebody to do things with. If it was any more serious than that, Mother never let on," she finished with a smile.

"May I see her father's letters?" I asked to change the subject.

"Of course. Why?"

"They may give me some insight into the situation. Or other relatives that I could talk to." Or why he never made contact with Viola again.

"Sure. We can run by my house on your way home."

Half an hour later, after much small talk, I followed her to her house, about fifteen minutes from the restaurant. She drove a cute sports car, red. It seemed to be the only nonconservative thing about her.

True to my expectations, she left half of her salad and ate ten bites of her manicotti. It was miraculous. She never lost any lipstick, and no food clung to the crevices in her perfect teeth.

I couldn't help but wonder if it was painful to live like that.

Her house was a large two-story, with a three-car garage, in Webster Groves, which is one of the more expensive areas of St. Louis County to live. The inside was as immaculate and symmetrical as her lawn had been. Neutral browns, beiges, and an occasional splash of salmon dominated her color scheme. Everything was wide open and her furniture was sparse. Probably on purpose, to add to the effect of having tons of room.

Within a few minutes she had gone to get a box containing her grandfather's letters.

"Thank you. I'll bring them back as soon as I've read them."

"Sure," she said.

The next thing I knew, I was being attacked by a killer Yorkshire terrier. The damned thing was yapping incessantly and biting my pants leg.

"What the . . . ?"

"Sparky, get down!" Rita ordered.

I've had dogs of my own and I'm usually the first to make friends with a stray. This little dog really unsettled me. I had never had a dog treat me this way.

"Sparky!" Rita finally corralled the little devil and set him outside. "God, I'm sorry. It's my mother's dog and he does that to everybody! He does it to me when I first come home, and I live here."

"How nice . . ." Suddenly I realized what she had just said. "Your mother's dog?"

"Yes."

"Did Sheriff Brooke ask you about the dog?"

"Yes, as a matter of fact. I told him that Jeff picks the dog up on Thursdays."

"Why?"

"Shots. He takes him to the vet to get his allergy shots. Mom couldn't bear to see the needle go in. Or hear him yelp for that matter. It was just a little errand he did for Mom." She smiled, face flushing. "Now I don't know what to do with it."

"Hmm," was all I managed.

That little errand that Jeff did for his mother could have aided in her death. If that dog reacted like that to all people, it could have warned her that somebody was in her house. Those stupid, trivial things that can put the wheels in motion were enough to drive me crazy.

Six

The rain poured from the skies as if there were no tomorrow. It was one of those perfectly puky days, like I remember as a kid. I'd sit in the classroom and stare at the windows as the rain slid down the glass, dripping off of the metal.

Rain in school didn't seem real. The sky turned dark, and the classroom followed into its murky shade. It gave the classroom an eerie feeling.

That is how I felt at the moment. I had caught my usual spring cold, brought on by allergies. My head felt as though it had been bludgeoned with a rubber sledgehammer, and my nose was raw. I had taken some over-the-counter sinus medication, which I should know better than to do. My legs were jumpy, and I could actually feel my hair growing. And I still had a stopped-up nose.

I had read every letter that Eugene Counts had written to Viola Pritcher. I had gleaned a few new names to check out, but nothing earth-shattering.

I had also received the death certificate for Eugene's mother, Edith Mae Chappuis Counts. I was really excited about this. Most people get excited over new cars; I get excited over death certificates. It's no wonder my husband worries about my state of mind.

Edith Mae Chappuis Counts was born in 1899. Her parents were Gaston Chappuis, born in France, and Ellenore Rousson, born in Ste. Genevieve County, Missouri. The certificate told the date, time, and place of death. I couldn't read who the attending physician was. But the most interesting piece of information was the informant. It was one Louise Mary Shenk, living in Washington, Missouri. This was Edith's daughter.

Who better than Eugene's own sister to talk to? She could give me some idea if Eugene would like to see Rita and Jeff.

Armed with new information, I headed downtown to the St. Louis library. I probably shouldn't have driven in my state of disorientation, but I couldn't let my sinuses rule my life.

The library, located on Olive Street, is a massive structure with about forty steps up the front of it. The ceilings are ornate, and huge marble pillars are everywhere. I think they even stuck them in places they didn't need to be. The history and genealogy room is quite impressive, as is the microfilm room downstairs.

I found a corner of the genealogy room and set up my pencils, paper, and briefcase. My first stop was back out to the center room, where the majority of the computers are. This is the information area, complete with a desk full of employees to retrieve books from the stacks.

One computer, however, has the telephone and address directory for the United States. If the person's unlisted or listed under another name, it's not much help.

I punched a bunch of keys until the computer was ready to take my request. I typed: Louise Shenk, Washington, Missouri. No Louise. Next I tried just the last name, Shenk, and the same city and state.

There were four Shenks living in Washington and I printed them all. They were all men and one could have been Louise's husband.

I went back to the history and genealogy room, scanned the wall that had the books on Missouri, and pulled out a copy of *Ste. Genevieve County Marriages 1870–1900*. Eugene's mother was born in 1899, so I assumed that her parents were married sometime between 1870 and 1899. Sure enough, they were married in 1896. So I filled that blank in on Norah's chart and went to make a copy of the page.

Next I pulled out the census index for Missouri for the year 1870. I assumed that Ellenore and Gaston were born before 1870. If I could find them in the census, then I'd know who their parents were. The index gave me the households in Ste. Genevieve County with the last names Chappuis and Rousson. I copied the page numbers and headed down to the microfiche and microfilm room.

I found them both, and thus added their birth years, and their parents' names and birth years, to Norah's chart. This is how the majority of the day went.

Six hours later I walked out of there with red eyes and a tense neck. But I had also nearly filled in Norah's five-generation chart. All in all it was a good day, except for having to run up and down all of those steps to feed the parking meter. It's no wonder people don't go to the library. It is too much work.

When I reached New Kassel, it was nearly time for dinner. I drove down Stuckmeyer Road and passed the Old Mill Stream, which is a restaurant now. It used to be a mill, hence the name. It still has its big wheel that took water from Kassel Creek. Mayor Castlereagh owns it now, and it was packed with customers.

I turned left and passed the three streets until I came to my driveway. There was a strange car parked in it, which was not all that unusual, but I wasn't expecting anybody, and I didn't recognize it. Somehow, I always feel on the defensive when I enter my own home with a stranger awaiting my arrival.

My house is white with green shutters, with a large front and back porch. Once I was inside my house, the aroma of my mother's sauerkraut, sausage, potato cakes, and baked beans sent my stomach into fits. I tripped over Mary's rocking horse, and let out a few expletives. The television blared, Dark Wing something or other, and that aggravated the heck out of me. One big rule in my house is no television during meals. Nobody talks to each other if the TV's on.

I turned it off with my thigh—yes, I'm one of the few cavemen without a remote control—and stopped dead in the doorway.

Sheriff Colin Brooke sat at *my* table, with *my* family, eating what was assuredly *my* dinner. He was charming the socks off of my mother, and even had Rudy laughing and pounding his hand on the table at something that was just "too funny."

Before I could utter something completely rude and justified, my mother interceded. "Victory, Sheriff Brooke . . ."

"Ms. Keith, call me Colin," he said, smiling at her.

"Oh, pah-leeze!" I said. "What is this?"

"We have a guest," Mom said.

"Mom," Rachel said. "Mom," she repeated, like all six-year-olds do when you don't answer them at the speed of light. My kids expect me to answer them before they ask the question!

"What?"

"He has a gun," she said, her black eyes huge.

As if I needed to hear that.

"Mother," I began, "you should be more careful who you invite to our house," I said. She glared at me.

"What do you want?" I asked him. I wouldn't get any prizes for being subtle. Sometimes subtlety only causes confusion.

We have only four kitchen chairs, so I grabbed a chair from the dining room as I picked up a potato cake and ate it. Sheriff Brooke watched me, his eyes trying desperately to communicate silently.

"He called first," Mom assured me. "To say he was coming, so I had him come for dinner." June Cleaver had just invaded my mother's body. I couldn't help but feel that I was missing something.

Rudy was being himself. He was genuinely entertained by Brooke. Rudy could not see beyond the surface of the dust on the mantel, much less the surface of people. Had they all forgotten my ill feelings for the sheriff? Had they all forgotten that this man threw me in jail when I was trying to get a pregnant woman to a hospital?

"Forgive my wife," Rudy said. "Hormones."

I swatted Rudy a good one on the side of his head. "I don't have hormones, dear. Not any! I don't have any!"

Obviously, they all believed me.

Mary took that opportune time to fling her sauerkraut across the table, hitting Sheriff Brooke in the head. I wanted to yell, "Good shot!" but I played the part of mother and reprimanded her. Even if it was done with a smile.

"So, Sheriff," I said, "what brings you to my house?"

"It can wait until we are finished eating," he said.

"Well, you'll be waiting forever, because my mother makes sure everybody is stuffed, and then she serves dessert. It's quite an ordeal," I said.

"One that I'm suffering through quite nicely," he answered.

Was he flirting with my mother? No, surely not. She was at least twelve years older than he.

Sheriff Brooke never spoke another word as to why he was at my house until we were completely finished with dinner. It was dusk now, but still light enough to see. Lavender was the primary color in the evening sky and the smell of grass and fresh rain had coiled themselves together. It had stopped raining about five that evening, but the local news assured us of more.

My backyard is large. We are on a two-acre lot. Over half of it is in the back of the house. Sheriff Brooke and I walked along the brick path that was lined with impatiens. All was calm and serene.

Suddenly Bob came squawking across the backyard. Bob is our rooster. He never hesitated as he headed straight for Sheriff Brooke's ankles. He pecked and squawked, and pecked some more. Sheriff Brooke tried desperately to get away from Bob without actually kicking him. He jumped on one foot, then on the other. He skipped along the sidewalk into the yard, back onto the sidewalk and then back into the yard, all the while throwing his feet out away from Bob. He looked like Michael Jackson doing a hoedown.

"Sorry," I muttered. "The chicken coop isn't quite finished." I swatted at Bob and then stomped my foot. "Go on, Bob, get."

I couldn't help but smile. And then I giggled. And then before I knew it, I was laughing heartily. "He has this thing about strange males. It's a dominance thing."

"It's all right," he said, cautious of every step he took. After all, there were a lot of things one could step into in my back-yard. "I'm surprised Bill hasn't made you get rid of the chick-ens. And the rooster," he said.

"You know the mayor?"

"Yeah."

He didn't say how or where from, just "Yeah." "He's tried," I said, "but we're not breaking any laws. I suppose you know that he hates anything furry or feathery."

"Yeah," he said as he shoved his hands in his jeans. "I didn't want you to have to come to the station so I could talk with you," he finally said. "I thought this would be better."

Something was bothering him. I don't think I have ever seen him quite so reflective. At least not around me.

"Did you know she was divorced?" he said.

"Yes," I said. "Have you talked to him?"

"Yesterday. He's a strange sort. Lives in Ladue. Recluse."

"Oh," I said. Ladue was one of the wealthiest parts of St. Louis County. A person could drop eight hundred thousand dollars on a home easily.

"Rita told me you were doing a family tree for her?" he asked.

"I told you that the day . . . the day she was killed. You weren't interested. Why now?" I asked, worried.

He looked up at the stars and breathed deeply. It was a cleansing breath, I thought. One that came from the bottom of the lungs. I wondered what it must be like to have to deal with death, Norah's kind of death, on any regular basis.

"Rita said something about Norah's dad?"

He finally got to the point he had been trying to make.

"She never met him. I found out that he was still alive; she thought he was dead. Why?"

"So she never talked to him?" he asked, discouraged.

"I never got the chance to tell her where he was," I said, un-sure of where this was going.

"Have you talked to him?" he asked.

"No. I didn't know how he would react. I was going to ask his sister first. I figure if the guy has never bothered to even see if Viola was breathing, there may be a reason."

"Can I have his sister's address?" he asked.

"Do you think that's wise?"

"I don't think that's for you to say. This is my investigation. I want to talk to his sister."

"I just thought that you might really shake the woman up. She doesn't even know Norah exists. So you're going to go to her house and tell her she had a niece that's been murdered, and her brother is a suspect, all in one visit. It just seems . . . cruel or something."

"I don't give a damn how it seems," he said. "Somebody butchered that woman, and I don't know where to start."

"Random," I remember thinking out loud.

"What?"

It was early enough in the year that it still got chilly when the sun set. I hugged myself tightly. "What if it was random?"

"Then I'm screwed. But I don't believe it was. There was nothing missing, no sexual assault. No forced entry." He again breathed deeply. "I'd say she was killed for a reason. Not random."

"What about fibers and such?" I asked.

"All kinds. We've got to have something to compare it to first," he said. "Anybody that's been in her house in the last few weeks will have left behind fibers and hairs anyway. I have to have a suspect first, and then compare fibers and hairs."

"What about John Murphy?" I asked, and was rather pleased with myself when it was clear he had no idea whom I was referring to.

"Something Rita said in passing to me at lunch the other day. She said that Norah had a boyfriend. One that she had been seeing for years, but had never married. I can't believe you didn't know about him," I said.

"Well, surprisingly, none of her neighbors knew she had a boyfriend. There was nothing in the house to indicate that there was a man that spent any amount of time there. And Jeff completely lied to me."

"What do you mean?"

"I asked him if his mother was seeing anybody and he said

no. I didn't bother asking Rita, because why would Jeff lie to me?" His question seemed to bother him the more he thought about it. "I even checked everybody's name that was on the register at the funeral."

Just then Mayor Castlereagh appeared over the top of the fencing, on a ladder. He pretended to be pruning a tree. At seven in the evening? It wasn't even the season to prune anything. All I could see of him was his bald head. Finally, he waved. I waved back.

Tomorrow everybody in town would know that Sheriff Colin Brooke had been in my backyard. Who am I kidding? They would know it two counties away. Small towns seem to breed gossip based on completely innocent events.

If John Murphy had been seeing Norah for years, then why wouldn't he show up at the funeral? Guilt? Shame? How about the inability to look at his own handiwork? Evidently, Brooke wasn't ready to comment any further on the subject.

"How could an entire neighborhood not know that she had a boyfriend? Especially one that she has been seeing for years?" I asked.

"Maybe they never came across as a couple, and therefore when we asked if she had a boyfriend, they said no. I will tell you that she was very private and kept to herself."

"I'm planning a visit to Louise Shenk. You can come along if you like," I said. "If you think it will help your investigation."

"Who?" he asked.

"Norah's aunt. I'm going to go see her tomorrow."

"What time?" he asked.

❧

THE NEWS YOU MIGHT MISS
by Eleanore Murdoch

The local quilters of the River Point Quilting Bee would like to announce that their quilt "Mississippi Heritage" took second place at the Midwest Quilt Fair. Congratulations, ladies! Oops, and Elmer Kolbe—I always forget he quilts. Raffles for two new quilts of theirs can be bought at the Quilt Supply on New Bavaria Boulevard. "Mississippi Heritage" can be seen on display at the Murdoch Inn.

Also, what's this I hear? Our sheriff had dinner with the O'Shea's? I'm open for more information.

Tobias still hasn't had his beloved statue of Abraham Lincoln returned. He's getting hotter than a snake in the Mojave Desert. (His words, not mine.)

The nuns at the Santa Lucia Catholic Church were presented with trees to plant. The trees were donated by Mrs. Hudsucker's kindergarten class. The trees came from the Wisteria nursery. Any great news? Write to me in care of the Murdoch Inn. Until next time.

Eleanore

Seven

I walked along Jefferson Street in an attempt to get to the Gaheimer House. I passed the lace shop with its low windows full of lace curtains and doilies. The Gaheimer House sits almost right on the sidewalk, its burnt brick overwhelming the passersby. The five windows and one door that are visible from Jefferson Street are painted in a yellow cream, surrounded by forest green shutters. It looks pretty sickening against the burnt-colored brick.

I stepped up on the wooden steps, and I was eye level with the plaque that reads, "Gaheimer House 1864." Sylvia Pershing met me at the front door. She didn't say a word. She only looked at me with her eyebrows knit together.

"Hello, Sylvia," I said as I walked by her. I heard her footsteps behind me as I passed through the parlor and then through the ballroom on my way back to the office. She was ticked about something.

Wilma waited for me in the office, sitting calmly, ankles and hands crossed. I had no idea what I had done wrong this time.

"Victory!" Sylvia's shrill voice sounded from ten feet behind me. She shut the door behind her and stood across from the desk. It was quite clear that she thought I had some explaining to do, but I had no idea what it was that I had to explain.

"Where are the marriage records for Granite County, 1850 to 1865?"

"Damn," I mumbled.

"Don't you dare use profanity in the Gaheimer House."

"It's not a church, Sylvia." Sometimes I think Sylvia has an unhealthy outlook on Hermann Gaheimer. The man died in 1930. Sylvia was in her twenties. She couldn't possibly have known him well enough to give him the sainthood that she most fervently thinks he deserved. but I figure I should keep such observations to myself.

"If you think you can answer my question without cursing, please do so," she said. "I'd love to hear your excuse for this one. Did your chickens eat them? Did Mary stuff them in your fish tank?"

"Sylvia, I know you'll never believe me, but Mary really did feed the fish the land records that I was working on." That was two years ago, and I hadn't been forgiven yet.

"Well? Where are the marriage records?"

"I haven't got them finished. Easy as that. No big conspiracy, I just don't have them finished. I have had a lot on my mind."

"Yes, like Colin Brooke?"

"Just what is that supposed to mean?"

"The whole county knows that you and he were talking in your backyard last night. Really, Victory. With your husband and children right inside."

"Oh, Sylvia . . ." I debated whether I should tell her that he was hitting on my mother. I suppose to her generation, any time two people of the opposite sex are in a backyard alone, that is a sign of something fishy. "He wanted to talk about the case."

"The case?" Wilma asked.

"Norah Zumwalt. He wanted to discuss a few things, that's all."

"And you had to do that in the romantic moonlight?" Sylvia asked.

"There was no moon last night," I answered.

"I think the butler did it," Wilma said.

"She didn't have a butler," I stated. Why did I feel as if I were in a zoo? "I just came by to get a file that I left here the other day."

Just then a horn sounded out on Jefferson Street.

"Who would that be?" Sylvia asked.

"Oh, that's probably the sheriff. He and I are driving out to Washington this morning," I said, and picked up the file and walked out of the office. I confess. It is a great perversion of mine to shock little old ladies.

"I'll get you your marriage records, Sylvia. I promise," I said, heading back through the ballroom and eventually out onto the sidewalk, where Sheriff Brooke waited for me in his yellow Festiva.

Everybody on the street stopped to look at me as I got in his car. People stood in the windows of the shops on the street and watched me. Heck, I think even the dead over in the Santa Lucia cemetery were watching.

I shook my head as we pulled away from the Gaheimer House and took off for Washington, Missouri.

It was a pleasant day, the sky was azure, and the foliage was bursting with life. These kinds of days erase all of the ugly things that fill one's life. Life is tricky. It lulls you into a false sense of beauty and hope, and then hits you with lightning.

The drive out Highway 44 was nice, if not enjoyable. Basically, we talked about how I got involved in genealogy and history. Some people find it hard to believe that a "young" person can be interested in those sorts of things. I suppose a greater percentage of family historians probably are over forty. But there are a great many young people just as enthusiastic about their heritage.

I had called the four numbers that I had, until I figured out which one was Louise Shenk. Finding her house was easy. It was a cute little two-story white bungalow, complete with a porch swing and roses. The yard was perfect and completely cluttered with several blooming plants.

My stomach was jittery. I'd never done anything like this before. Sheriff Brooke exuded calm. He walked with an air of superiority, his shoulders thrown back. He was close to forty. He was by no means ugly, but not exactly handsome either. It would be difficult, I knew, for him to take the backseat during our visit.

I rang the doorbell and waited. A robust old woman answered the door. Her eyes were bright, and the hair that wasn't white was of a dark color.

"Louise Shenk?" I asked. I gave a big, bright smile.

"Yes," she answered, unsure and out of breath.

"Hi, my name is Victory O'Shea. I'm tracing the Counts family tree, of southeast Missouri. Could you answer a few questions for me?"

She hesitated, looking from Sheriff Brooke back to me. I sensed her unease. "We can sit here on the porch. Just a few minutes."

She took the chair on the front porch and motioned for Sheriff Brooke and me to take the swing.

"This is Colin Brooke," I said. "A friend."

They nodded at each other, and that was it. Each one was measuring the other. My tape recorder was running in my pocket, and I had my notebook and pen ready.

"Mrs. Shenk, I've been working on the Counts family tree for a couple of months—"

"How are you related?" she asked quickly.

"I'm not, directly. I was hired to do it." I shifted through my notes, making it look as though I had to look something up. "Could you tell me what your father did for a living?"

"He was a farmer, and a Methodist minister. . . . He had several churches that he preached at: New Mullen, Avon, Pine Branch."

"Pine Branch? My great-grandpa helped build that church," I said, genuinely surprised. "Back in 1912. He was about twenty then."

"Well, my lands!" she exclaimed. Don't ask me what that phrase means. My grandfather was always full of what I call Americanisms. One of his favorites was "The dickens, you say." I don't think he had any idea what it meant.

"That was actually the second time that church had been built," she went on. "The original burned."

Sheriff Brooke rolled his eyes, as if he didn't believe a word of what I or she was saying. "Anything else you can tell me about

55

him would be a great help. Anything interesting?"

"One time, we housed a band of Gypsies for the night. Mama thought for sure that they were gonna steal us blind. Next morning the only thing they'd took was my little brother," she said. "Dad rode for hours at a hard run to catch 'em. That was when we only had the two horses, and both were old and you had to lean 'em up against a fence post when you weren't using them. We was real worried that he would kill Bertha riding her that hard."

Her breath was labored, and she stopped several times in between words. I found myself being overly aware of every breath I took, in reaction to her labored breathing.

"When Papa caught up to them, he asked them how come they took his son? They said they didn't take him, they let him come along," she said. She laughed at the memory of it. "Them Gypsies have unique ways of saying things."

"Your little brother? Would that have been Eugene?"

"No, Bobby," she said. "There was Ruthie, me, Bobby, Eugene, and Edith," she said. She marked each one with one of her fingers.

"Now Eugene, he fought in the war, right? World War II?" I asked, and hoped that I wasn't too obvious.

"Yes," she answered. She showed no outward emotion at the mention of this. She only looked from me to Sheriff Brooke.

"Where was he stationed?"

"All over Europe, you know . . . France, Germany, not sure."

"Did he ever get married?" I asked as I wrote everything down.

"Not to my knowledge. Though he was going to once," she said. "Sweet girl, named Viola."

Norah's mother, I thought. I had filled Sheriff Brooke in on Norah's family tree, so at the mention of Viola, he sat to attention.

"Do you know why he didn't marry her?" Brooke asked.

"No," she said.

I cleared my throat, unable to say what it was I really wanted to say to her. How do you ask somebody if her brother got his

56

girlfriend pregnant? Nowadays it isn't that big a thing. But for her generation, it would be improper for me to just ask that sensitive a question.

"Did he have any children?"

"No, but I often suspected that Viola might have been carrying," she said with no emotion. "She moved up to St. Louis shortly after he went to war. She'd come down now and then to see Mama, but she came alone and we only saw her once a year, maybe."

"For how long?"

"Just a couple of hours."

"No, I mean how many years did she do this?"

"Till Mama died."

Till Mama died?

That thought was heartbreaking. To think that Viola went to see Eugene's mother every year until she died. Why? Was she secretly wishing that Edith Counts would ask her if she had given birth to Eugene's child? Or was it that she was still hoping that somebody would tell her something of him, after all of those years? Her loyalty was admirable. All of that time, even though she had married somebody else, she still waited for somebody to tell her what had become of him, or why he'd dumped her.

"Mrs. Shenk, I will be honest with you. Viola did have a child by Eugene. A daughter. It was her daughter who hired me to trace his family tree," I said, still shocked that I just came out and said exactly what I was thinking. After all, I usually do say what I'm thinking, but not when I know it could hurt somebody this badly.

I suppose I expected her either to fall out of her chair or throw us off of the porch. She did neither. She only smiled to herself, at some inward thought or memory.

"Not surprised," she said.

"I'm sorry for the deception, but I wasn't sure how you would take being told that you had a niece that you knew nothing about."

She waved a hand toward me. "It's okay."

"Well, the real reason I came to visit," I said, delighted at her willingness to talk, "is that Norah, his daughter, had been wanting to meet with him. How do you think he would react to that?"

"Don't know," she said. "Ask him, if you can find him."

I glanced over at Sheriff Brooke; both of us realized the hidden definition in her statement.

"What do you mean, if we can find him?" asked Sheriff Brooke. A muscle in his jaw flexed as he prepared to pounce on any shred of evidence.

She played with her wedding band, contemplating an answer. When she finally looked up at me, her eyes were filled with tears. "I've not laid eyes on him since he walked up the dirt road in front of Mama's house. He walked to town to catch a bus to go fight Hitler," she said. Her voice was quiet with pain. "He never came back. He wrote to us for a while. He wasn't killed and he wasn't missing in action. He survived the war. But he never came home."

I was stunned. "Do you mean to tell me that he came back to America and never even came to see his mother?"

"He might have stayed in Europe. But, yes to your question. He never saw Mama, and it killed her. One day she told me that she had failed as a mother, because no good son would do that to their mama. She had accepted the fact he'd never come home. The day that she accepted it, she died on the inside. The life ran out of her."

I didn't know if Eugene had lived in Vitzland at the time of his mother's death or not. But how was I supposed to tell Louise that he could have lived there the whole time and never gone to see his mother? They had been nursing the idea that maybe he just never came back from Europe. I could burst that bubble for her, too.

"They say that war changes a man," she said coldly. "But enough to walk away from his family? Enough to walk away from his mama? Everything that he knew and loved?"

She was bitter, and I didn't blame her. I was so angry with

Eugene Counts, I could have strangled him, and I was no relation.

"Where is he at?" she asked, surprising Sheriff Brooke as much as me. "You wouldn't have asked how he would feel about meeting his daughter if you didn't know where he was," she said.

I had to be honest with her. She was entitled. She was also very perceptive, and I couldn't have got by with trying to lie my way out of it.

"Vitzland," I said, ashamed for Eugene.

Saying nothing, she stood and disappeared into her house. I shrugged at Sheriff Brooke, thinking that was the end of our interview. She returned, however, just as Brooke and I had stood to leave, with a photo album. She flipped through it, pulling out a few photos as she went. It was as if she had the photo album memorized. She knew what photos were on what page.

"Give these to his daughter," she said. "I have no use for them anymore."

I stared sullenly at the pile of photographs. I had brought her such pain this day and I felt guilty as hell. Who did I think I was, that I could just waltz up to somebody's doorstep and pour salt in her wounds?

"She died, Mrs. Shenk," I said. "His daughter died." After everything else that she had learned today, I wasn't going to tell her that Norah had been murdered. "But I will give them to Norah's daughter."

"Thank you," was all that she said. "I'm tired."

I took that as a cue to leave. Before I stepped off of her porch, I stopped and met her eyes. "I am truly sorry," I said.

"So am I."

We were halfway to our car when Sheriff Brooke stopped and went back to the foot of the steps. It reminded me of how he had done that to me, the day that Norah had been killed. I knew the detective in him wouldn't let him leave without asking her some police type of question. There was too much potential with this character witness, too much that he could learn from her.

"Ma'am," he began. "Do you have any idea what changed

him? Do you think that maybe he had been deformed in the war? You know, too embarrassed to come home?"

"No. I can't say for sure, but he had a friend in the same unit. He was a native of Ste. Genevieve County. I think maybe he had an influence on Eugene. But not enough to change a boy that was as good as Eugene. He was such a good boy," she said. Her breathing grew steadily worse. Her chest rose rapidly and I didn't know if it was from asthma or something like congestive heart failure. Either way, we had bothered her enough.

Sheriff Brooke watched as she made it safely inside her door. I heard everything they had said, not being more than a few feet behind the sheriff.

"You drive," he said.

"Why?"

"I want to write some notes," he said. "While they're still fresh."

When we were in his car, I adjusted the mirror and his seat.

"If something changed a man enough that he never came to visit his mother ever again, do you think it could make him a murderer?" he asked.

I think the sheriff was simply thinking out loud to himself, rather than asking me directly, but I decided to answer him just in case. "Normally, I might agree with your line of thinking. But Eugene Counts didn't even know about Norah. He did not know that he had a child," I answered.

"How do we know he didn't?" he asked with a "let's get 'em" look.

"Is that it? Case closed? A man doesn't come home to his family after the war and that makes him a butcher of his own daughter?" I was furious with him, even though I secretly thought back to the newspaper ad that Norah had placed. Could he have seen it? Could he have known that she existed? But so what if he had seen the ad? Why kill her?

Something in me wanted to find an excuse for Eugene.

"What if he had a reason? Like some illegal reason. He didn't want anybody to know where he was, and she found out?" Sheriff Brooke asked.

60

"Then why move back to Missouri at all? Why not stay in Europe? Why not Florida or Arizona, where it's warm all the time?" I argued.

He looked at me as if I were the stupidest thing to walk on two feet.

"What about the ex-husband?" I asked.

"He's clean," he said in a matter-of-fact tone.

"What you mean to say is, he is an untouchable," I said as I started the engine. I slammed the car into reverse and then forward again once we were out in the street. I enjoyed watching his head snap back and forth.

"I'm not stupid," I said at the stop sign. "I'm very aware of who Zumwalt is."

"Who?" he asked.

"Harold Zumwalt, of Zumwalt and Macklintock. A big-shot law firm, and I'm guessing you've been told to lay off."

The cars behind me had lined up, waiting for me to go. They were honking, so I obliged them. I gunned the car and watched Sheriff Brooke's head snap back on the headrest once again.

Grabbing the steering wheel, he pulled the car over to the shoulder. "You do that one more time," he said with an eerie calmness, "and I will write you a list of citations as long as the Gettysburg Address."

"We know how you love to write citations that aren't earned," I snapped back.

"What made you say that?"

"Don't pretend that you don't remember giving me that ticket and throwing me in jail. Everything is so cut-and-dried to you."

"Not that, the other."

"What?"

"About laying off of Zumwalt."

"A hunch," I said.

He glanced out the passenger window. His jaw worked nervously as he rubbed his thumb across his eyebrow. He pulled a piece of chewing gum out of his pants pocket. He must be trying to quit smoking, I decided.

61

"I wasn't told to lay off," he said, aggravated. "But I did receive a very nasty phone call from his lawyers, stating that he had an alibi for the day and night before. And not to push things any further."

"Why would they do that?" I asked.

"That doesn't matter. It's the fact that Zumwalt's name arouses many different people from many walks of life. I have to be careful with him until I can prove something beyond a doubt."

"So the part about him being a hermit isn't exactly the truth, is it?"

"Actually, he is a recluse socially. He never goes out any more than necessary, unless it is job related."

I was suddenly hit with hunger pains, and my stomach growled on cue. I was happy that Sheriff Brooke had shared information from the case with me. I wasn't stupid though. I knew that there were all sorts of tidbits that I would never be made privy to. I also knew that the little bit of information that he'd just told me wasn't something "top secret" or desperately important to catching a killer. "What reason would he have to kill her?" I asked finally.

He thought a moment and then answered. "None."

I doubted that, but I left it alone anyway. Beggars can't be choosers, and if he didn't want to elaborate on his thoughts where Zumwalt was concerned, I certainly couldn't force him. Mr. Zumwalt was indeed a powerful man with long arms.

In ten minutes, we were on Highway 44 and on our way home.

Eight

I stood on the small swell of the River Point Road levee. The
Mississippi had doubled in size in the past two weeks. We were
in big trouble.

"I've never seen it quite this high," a voice said.

I glanced over my shoulder to see Chuck Velasco leaning on
his shovel. He is a good old boy, and I don't mean that in a
derogatory way. He wears cowboy boots, always. I've never seen
him in a pair of tennis shoes. He had on Levi's and a muscle shirt.
I, on the other hand, was dressed in tennis shoes and shorts, and
a T-shirt that advertised a local radio station. Chuck is about
thirty-five, with reddish hair and brown eyes. He is the owner of
Velasco's Pizza, and we've known each other since we were kids.

"Can't say that I have either," I said.

Shovels pierced the piles of sand directly behind me. The
swish sound that they made seemed to flood my ears. See, we in
the community of New Kassel were in particularly irritated
moods. We had a lot to lose if the levee broke. Not just our
homes, but our livelihoods. Our entire town was a commodity.

We didn't have a whole lot of breathing room either. My
home, half a dozen others, the Murdoch Inn, the Birk/Zeis
Home, Ye Olde Train Depot, and the Old Mill Stream were separated from the waters of the Mississippi by River Point Road
and the levee.

And so we sandbagged. Sheriff Brooke sandbagged just two
feet away from me.

63

"Where's Rudy?" Chuck asked me.

"He's down at Ye Olde Train Depot, bagging his heart away," I said.

"Well, let's give some of these people a break," Chuck said.

Sylvia and Wilma were foremen of the sandbagging project. They stood close by on the porch of the Murdoch Inn.

Chuck filled the bags with sand, and I carried them over to the sandbag wall and piled them on. An hour later we switched. I filled and he carried. The blisters on my feet were burning, but not nearly as much as the blisters on my hands. My neck was tense, and I felt like the Hunchback of Notre Dame from being in a bent position too long.

"I sure am glad my house is on a hill," I said to Chuck.

"Yeah. You probably won't have to bag there at all. If the water gets up that high, I'm building me an ark."

"Victory!" Sylvia yelled. "Don't fill the bags too full."

"Yes, Sylvia." Why did it seem like those were the two words I spoke the most?

"If that old biddy doesn't shut up I'm going to shove a sandbag right up—"

"Chuck," I said. "No need in getting violent."

Chuck is about the nicest guy in the whole town, except when it comes to Sylvia Pershing. He, like many of the townspeople, has no patience or tolerance for her. It always seems as if I am interceding on her behalf.

"She really gripes me," Chuck said as he glared at Sylvia standing on the porch of the Murdoch Inn.

"If it weren't for Sylvia Pershing, this town would be just a sorry river town, with no commerce whatsoever and nothing to be proud of," I said.

"Humph," he responded as he carried off a bag and placed it on top of the others. There were at least fifteen other baggers at the Murdoch Inn. They were all moaning as well. Chuck came walking back. "What makes her be such a sourpuss? Wilma isn't like that."

"Well," I said as I pushed my shovel into the sand pile, "I'm not sure. But she is pretty much single-handedly responsible for this town. She took her own money and restored all of these buildings. I can even remember her giving loans to people to start businesses in them."

He shrugged as I filled the bag he held open. "But the really great part is, she didn't charge anybody interest on those loans. All you had to do was pay her back, exactly what you borrowed. And I can name at least seven people that she helped in that way," I said. I stopped to lean on my shovel and wipe the sweat from my brow on my T-shirt.

The baggers got rather quiet and stopped shoveling. I turned around and saw why. Deputy Newsome was headed, as determined as he could possibly look, toward the sheriff.

I glanced up at the porch of the Murdoch Inn. It is the only bed-and-breakfast in the town, and one of the most gorgeous buildings. Only about a hundred years old, it was built in the early 1890s, with two turrets and a wraparound porch that is adorned with latticework and spiral decorations. It is white with two stories, and an attic that houses the two most adorable rooms in the whole building.

However, all I could see at the moment was Sylvia's glare as she watched Sheriff Brooke put down his shovel and prepare to speak with his deputy.

It had been a week since Brooke and I visited with Louise Shenk, and I'd done nothing with the photos or information she'd given me. I had heard through the grapevine that the sheriff had a few other important things to do and that he'd put Deputy Newsome on the case doing his footwork. I wondered when Sheriff Brooke was going to visit Eugene Counts and if he would take me along. Probably not, I thought to myself. If I wanted to talk to Eugene, I'd have to go by myself.

"Hello, Colin," Deputy Newsome said.

"What is it, Newsome?" the sheriff said with a nod.

"I got some news for you," Newsome said.

The sheriff looked around and saw Sylvia giving him the evil eye, and decided that Newsome could tell him what he wanted right there. I must admit that I was relieved at this, because I was hoping to overhear a bit of it.

Everybody else went back to what they were doing, and Sylvia came off the porch to stand at the foot of the steps, hoping to get within hearing distance as well. Is this where I was headed? Someday would I take over Sylvia's throne? I'd have to work on the scowl.

"Zumwalt had a seven-hundred-fifty-thousand-dollar life insurance policy on Norah," the deputy said to the sheriff.

I dropped the shovel, then tried desperately to recover it and pretend as though I'd dropped it from fatigue only. Sheriff Brooke gave me a funny look, but said nothing. It was incomprehensible. Could it be that simple? Could Zumwalt have killed her for the insurance money?

"Before or after?" Sheriff Brooke asked as I picked up the shovel.

"Before or after what?" Deputy Newsome asked.

"The divorce. When was the policy taken out?" the sheriff asked.

"Years before the divorce," Newsome answered. He sounded disappointed.

"He could have been biding his time. You know, so nobody would get suspicious," Brooke said.

"Oh, and the information on John Murphy," Newsome stated.

"Yeah?"

I was about ready to say "Yeah?" along with the sheriff. I hate it when people dangle their sentences like that.

"He's some sort of broker or something. I don't know anything about those types of jobs," the deputy said, annoyed. "But the really interesting thing is, he doesn't have an alibi for the last two days of the week when Norah was killed. He got back in town on Wednesday from a business trip and wasn't seen again until Saturday morning at his golf course. But something else—he and Norah both had life insurance policies on each other."

"What?"

"That's right. The only problem is that they aren't worth very much. I can't believe a man like John Murphy would kill Norah for fifty thousand dollars."

"Victory! Get moving!" Sylvia yelled.

I jumped. I had forgotten that I was supposed to be filling the bag with sand, so involved was I in what Deputy Newsome was saying to the sheriff.

"Right, okay," I said, and complied. I wondered what he meant when he said a man like John Murphy.

Deputy Newsome sighed. "He's a regular average guy who makes a comfortable living," he stated. It was as if he'd heard me. "He happens to be an upstanding citizen. Not even a traffic violation. What I'm trying to say is, I could see this guy snapping for some reason and killing Norah. But not for fifty thousand dollars. It would have to have been personal."

"Maybe he was in debt with the wrong kind of people, and the only way he could think to get the money was from the insurance policies."

The sheriff hoisted a bag onto his shoulder and carried it over to the rapidly growing wall. The deputy followed him, and I had no idea what they said to each other for at least a minute. When the sheriff returned to his pile of sand, Deputy Newsome said, "If he's in debt, it's the kind that's off the record. His credit history is better than mine."

"Why have the insurance policies at all?" the sheriff asked.

"He says that whoever died first, between them, was to use the money to bury the other one in the fashion that they had already discussed. The policies didn't need to be very large just for that." He swiped at the fast-accumulating sweat on his brow. "Seems that her kids didn't want to conform to her burial wishes, and he had no children."

Sheriff Brooke looked up suddenly and waved over my shoulder. I turned around to see Rudy walking up behind me, exhausted and just as sweaty as I was. Rudy waved back.

"So the money was just to bury each other with?" Brooke asked.

"Looks like it. At least that's the story that John Murphy is telling me."

"Then why wasn't he at the funeral? Not only does he not take control of her funeral arrangements, he doesn't even show up at the funeral."

Exactly what I had been thinking.

Rudy kissed me on the cheek. He tried not to get too close. His sweat glands were working overtime. Missouri is one of the muggiest places in the United States. Nobody can visit here in the summer and not sweat buckets.

"I asked him that, too," the deputy said. "He claims—this is the part that is too hard to believe—he claims that he was not informed of Norah's death until everything was done and over with."

"Wow," I said.

They both looked over at me, now aware of my eavesdropping.

"Wow, it sure is hot," I said, trying to recover. I don't think it worked.

The sheriff looked me right in the eye then and asked, "Anything new on the family-tree side of things?"

"Hmm? Oh, no. Not yet," I said, my mind elsewhere.

"Well, I think I might do some off-the-record digging on Mr. Zumwalt," he said as he turned back to Deputy Newsome. He lowered his voice a bit. "I think he is my best target at the moment."

"All right," Newsome said. "I'm gonna send some people over from Wisteria to help you guys sandbag."

"You do that," the sheriff said.

"I'm exhausted," I said to Rudy. "Let's go home and take a shower."

"Sounds heavenly," Rudy said to me.

"See ya later, Chuck. I'm going home."

Chuck smiled and nodded his head. At the last minute he added, "Rudy, come down and get a beer later."

Rudy nodded affirmative to him and I handed my shovel over to somebody on the sidelines who was refreshed. I had thought that there was a point when I was so exhausted that my mind would stop reeling. Evidently I hadn't reached it yet, because I kept wondering about the question the sheriff had asked me: *Anything new on the family-tree side of things?*

Nine

I felt very accomplished. The chicken coop was finished. We had put a twelve-foot-high fence around the wooden building, leaving the chickens a nice courtyard to do whatever it is chickens do. We had sandbagged until I thought we would drop, and for now, the river was being held. I had even finished the marriage records that I'd been working on for Sylvia.

I was standing in my office at home, staring at the box that Rita had given me. It contained, among other things, the letters from Eugene Counts. Since Louise had mentioned that he had a friend in the service, the letters took on new meaning. I began to scour them, looking for new names.

Two hours later, my eyes were crossed and my neck was stiff, but I had found several references to a private named Mike Ortlander. I jotted the name on the cover of her file, in big black letters, so that I could do some checking on him later.

Right now I smelled something cooking downstairs and I just had to go see what it was. If my nose was correct it was German chocolate cake.

I passed the kitchen and noticed a Jane Austen novel on the table. Mother was reading nineteenth-century literature. This could mean only one thing: She was disturbed.

The photos from Louise Shenk were on the table as well. I had debated taking them over to Rita, but somehow couldn't part with them just yet.

"Mom," Rachel said. "Will you read me a story?"

I started to say no, and realized that I had told the girls no on several occasions recently. The marriage records, the chicken coop, sandbagging, all had taken my time away from them. They wanted Mommy to pay special attention to them and it made me feel good.

"Certainly. Get your sister, and bring me a really good book."

"Which one?" she asked, eyes all lit up.

"You pick."

I cut three small pieces of cake and poured three large glasses of milk. Mary came running into the kitchen.

"I want some cake, Mommy. Mommy, I want some cake," she said.

"Don't worry. One of these pieces has your name on it."

She smiled from ear to ear. It's a contagious smile. I can never be in the same room with her when she smiles, and not smile myself.

Rachel came back in the kitchen, out of breath. "Here," she said, and handed me the book. *The Secret Garden*. I should have known. It was the old standby, and even Mary would sit and listen, completely enthralled.

"I'll read it as soon as we have our snack. Then you have to go to bed."

I received crestfallen faces and a huge sad sigh. Children know that they have to go to bed every night, so I never have been able to understand why they are so upset when they find out that they have to go to bed.

"Where's Dad?" Rachel said.

"Bowling. He should be home in a few minutes."

Mother came into the kitchen then. She had paint splatters on her face, which was a good indication that she had been out on the porch creating her latest masterpiece. She began painting a few years back, and was quite good at it. Sometimes, though, the canvas ends up in the trash can. I've told her that a temper tantrum is the true sign of genius. She just glares at me.

"Did you check out the names?" she asked.

"What names?"

"On the picture," she answered, pointing to the photographs from Louise Shenk on the table. One photo was of Eugene Counts as a small boy, standing by the outhouse, with no shoes, holding something in his hands. Another was a typical midwestern country-school photo with all fifteen students and the teacher lined up on the schoolhouse steps. He was about thirteen, so it was about 1936. Another photo was of his parents sitting in the front yard, and yet another of the whole family down by the creek, the boys in just their underwear, holding makeshift fishing poles, while the girls waded in the water with their dresses tied between their knees. The last two photos had been sent from Europe during the war.

I was touched when I realized that Louise had given such a wonderful collection to Rita. Each part of Eugene Count's life was represented in those few photographs.

The war photos were classic war photos. About ten men stood half-dressed in front of army tents. Each had his dog tags hanging on his sweaty chest, and some had cigarettes in their mouths. They were probably the closest of buddies that looked after each other and saved each other's lives a thousand times. They probably even had a secret handshake.

The last photo was of Eugene and another man. They were sitting on top of a tank, but it was a fairly close-up photo.

"Right there." Mom pointed.

I looked at her, dumbfounded. When I looked at the photo, I saw two faces. Somehow my mother saw two names that had been sewn on their shirts. One read E. COUNTS, and the other simply said ORTLANDER.

I could hit her when she does stuff like that. She always makes me feel completely inadequate in the brain department for not catching the same thing she did.

"Ortlander," I said. "This is the same guy that Eugene speaks of in his letters to Viola," I said. "This has got to be the friend that Louise was talking about."

"Probably," she said.

"I love you, Mom."

"I know," she said.

"What's all of this loving stuff?" Rudy asked from behind me. He had just come in the door with his bowling bag in one hand and daisies in the other hand.

"Can I get in on this?" he asked. He kissed me on the lips and handed me the flowers.

"Certainly," I said. I kissed him back, rather enthusiastically.

"Yuck," Rachel said.

"Yuck," Mary echoed her big sister.

THE NEWS YOU MIGHT MISS
by Eleanore Murdoch

Thank you, all you sandbaggers! God bless your generous souls! You've saved our inn, for now.

And a special thank you to Wilma Pershing for that terribly stinky, but very effective, conglomeration of *stuff* that I put on Oscar's back. It worked!

Also, Tobias Thorley would like to thank whoever it was that returned his statue of Abraham Lincoln. He is very glad that he appealed to your conscience, because he was going to resort to violence next.

Father Bingham said that church attendance is down. He knows that nobody here in New Kassel is without sin, and he urges you to come and spill your guts to him. He's reading the *National Enquirer* in the confessional, if that gives you any idea of what business is like. He would especially like to speak to the couple that he saw on the wharf last Friday night.

I just have one thing to say to that: What was Father Bingham doing on the wharf on Friday night?

Oh, and congratulations to Rudy O'Shea for finally getting your chicken coop finished.

Until next time.

Eleanore

Ten

I wanted to see Eugene Counts. I could think of no reason other than that I was nosy as hell, and I hoped that he would spill his guts and tell me just why he had never contacted his family. I wanted to know the answer to that more than anything. Why come back to Missouri and spend the majority of your life without contacting your own mother? I also wanted to know if he knew that Viola was pregnant when he marched off to war. I wanted to see his face when I asked these questions, but something told me to wait. I didn't think he would appreciate being told he had a daughter by the woman he abandoned, if in fact he didn't already know it. The nagging notion of him being a psychopathic killer kept me at bay somewhat, too.

So I checked the directories for 1939, for Ortlanders. I found a Walt Ortlander, who lived in Pine Branch, the same place that the Counts family had lived. In 1946, there was no listing for a Michael Ortlander and I could only presume that Louise had been correct when she said that Eugene's friend had died in the service. There was also no listing for Eugene Counts. He must have still been in Europe or living elsewhere.

I called information and there was no Walt Ortlander listed for this year. He'd probably be dead by now. I was striking out. But there was a listing for a Florence Ortlander in the Hill Top Nursing Home in Progress. I would almost bet that she was Michael's mother. I called the Hill Top Nursing Home and told them that I was a friend of the family and had lost contact with the Ortlanders, and asked if the Florence Ortlander that they had in residence was the wife of Walt. Yes, she was.

I was in the car and headed to Progress in nothing flat. Progress was located about nine or ten miles west of Pine Branch, thus putting it in Partut County.

The dirt roads weren't dusty. The rains had seen to that problem. I felt the tension leave my body the farther into the country that I drove. People consider New Kassel in the country, but it's a town. Wisteria, Meyersville, Vitzland, they are all towns, but they are connected by just two- or four-lane roads and cornfields. I suppose to a real city dweller that is the country.

But on the drive to Progress there were no skyscrapers to interfere with sky and earth, and the smell of cow manure floated heavily through the air. Aaah! It was good to be alive.

It took so little to make me happy.

Why did I bother with this? I couldn't help but think that somewhere, hidden in all of Norah's family skeletons, I might be able to find something that would help the sheriff out. He wouldn't be looking in the same places I'd be looking. And I wanted justice done to the monster that left Norah in the shape that I found her in.

In all probability, though, Harold Zumwalt killed Norah. Money was about as good a motive as any. There was always the possibility that Eugene Counts had killed his own daughter. But why? It lacked motive.

So why did I care about Michael Ortlander? I suppose I was going to go talk with Florence for other reasons. I wanted to know what had changed Eugene Counts. To me, that was more important right now than anything else. I felt as if I somehow owed Norah that much.

I couldn't help but feel as if I were missing something in all of this. If Zumwalt was going to kill his ex-wife for the insurance money, why so violently? There were a thousand other ways to do it.

Her murder had been an act of passion.

Saying a silent prayer that I would never know what drove

people to do things like that, I pulled off the interstate at the Progress exit. It had taken me forty minutes to get to Progress, but the time flew by thanks to my mind, which would not stop analyzing everything. I made a few turns and then turned into the nursing-home drive. I knew it well. I'd driven by it many times, and my great-grandmother had been here her last six months.

The woman behind the counter was Doris, and I could tell by looking that she could tell me all of the bedpan bylaws and codes, in complete detail and numerical order.

I hadn't exactly dressed for a visit. I was in my black Reeboks, blue jeans, and St. Louis Blues hockey jersey, with Brendan Shanahan's name and player number. Number nineteen. Hopefully Mrs. Ortlander would be a hockey fan.

Doris decided to pretend as though she couldn't see me. There is nothing more aggravating than to stand at a counter and be ignored. Doris knew I was standing there, but she was determined to make me say "Excuse me" in that meek little voice that throws you right back to second grade. I was just as determined not to say it. Why should I? What other reason could I possibly have for standing at her counter, other than that I needed her assistance?

I rolled my eyes, shifted my feet, and sighed as loudly as I could sigh, at least thirteen times. She finally looked up and with this droll attitude said, "Yes?"

I waited. I was half-inclined to make her wait for my request as she had made me wait for her assistance.

"What room is Florence Ortlander in, please?" I asked.

"Are you a relative?"

I didn't have to be a relative to see her—I knew that much. Doris was just being nosy. "I'm her niece," I said.

"She never mentioned you," she said, unimpressed.

Her eyes were hazel, although I could hardly tell for all of the makeup she wore. She was about fifty, and her hair looked like it had been teased back in 1965, and hadn't been brushed since then.

"She's around the corner, room one-seventeen," she said. She eyed me suspiciously.

"Thank you."

Rounding the corner, I became acutely aware of the smells of alcohol and pine cleaner. And urine. How come elderly people can live at home and you never smell those things? As soon as they go to a nursing home, the cherry pie, facial powder, and mothballs get replaced with urine and pine cleaner. It was sad and it made me nervous to meet Mrs. Ortlander. I hadn't thought of what kind of shape she would be in.

Luckily, Florence Ortlander was sitting in a chair crocheting, and other than being obviously well into her years, was the picture of health. I noticed the popcorn stitch immediately, as Mom uses it often. She glanced up and didn't seem the least bit concerned that a stranger had come to see her. She was small, with rosy cheeks and the clearest blue eyes I believed I had ever seen.

"Mrs. Ortlander, my name is Victory O'Shea," I said.

"Nice to meet you. Have a seat," she said.

I sat in the seat on the opposite side of the round table that she was sitting at. Before I could say anything else to her, she picked up the conversation.

"Where did you get a name like Victory?" she asked.

I hate answering that question. "Two reasons. One, I was a victory. My mother was told she'd never have children. She was victorious. Two, I was also named after a ghost." Most people are named after grandmothers or maiden aunts; I was named after a ghost.

"Victory LeBreau."

"Yes," I said, amazed. "The woman who burned to death in the old mill."

"I grew up in Avon. Moved to Pine Branch in the early thirties. Everybody knows the story of the ghost that haunts the mill very well. I saw her once, you know. I was about sixteen years old," she said. "I was coming home from a dance at the church. It was dark already, and me and my sister were going to get the tanning of our lives for being so late."

I was totally engrossed in what Mrs. Ortlander said. It didn't seem the least bit odd for her to talk to me as if she'd known me her entire life. That's how natural this story flowed out of her.

"Well, we came up on the bridge and Trula stopped in her tracks. She didn't have to tell me what was wrong, I could feel the gooseflesh on her arm. Then I heard it. The sobbing of a woman in the distance. It was a woeful cry. Then I heard her screaming, 'No! No!' Then we saw her. She flung herself at the window of the mill. Second floor, third window from the left. I'll never forget it."

"What happened then?" I asked.

"Well you know the mill is burned out now, one whole wall is missing. But for a split second I thought I saw the mill the way it used to be. Whole, with all four of its walls. Well, Victory Le-Breau stopped with her arms raised up over her head. She stopped and she looked right at me. She looked right into my soul."

She paused in her story then. I had goosebumps the size of dimes all down my arms.

"And? What happened?" I asked.

"She began pounding on the window, shouting for help. They say she relives her inferno every night."

"Yes, I have heard that," I said.

"You must be from the same area."

The woman was ninety-plus years and looked it. She had severe wrinkles and very white hair. But she was also alert, her voice strong, and her hands nimble. Between her and the Pershing sisters, I had the feeling that I was falling apart and wouldn't make it to forty.

"I'm from Progress, originally," I said. "My great-grandfather helped to build the Pine Branch church, and my grandparents lived there for many years. Have you heard of the Frioux family?"

"Yes. Claude had a daughter about eight years older than me. She was the prettiest thing I've ever seen. Always wanted to look like her."

"Felicity Frioux?"

"Yes."

"That was my grandmother," I said, suddenly somber and forgetting the real reason I'd come here.

"How nice," she said. "Do you crochet?"

"Sorry," I said. "I am all thumbs at that sort of thing."

She gestured at her hospital bed as she said, "Do you quilt?"

A gorgeous Lone Star quilt graced her bed. The Lone Star is made up of small diamonds pieced together in larger diamond sections that eventually make up the star. This one was done in different shades of mauve and pink. How out of place it looked in this sterile room, and on a hospital bed.

"Not unless collecting them counts," I answered her. "I have several quilt tops my grandmother left me."

"Well, you'd best get them quilted," she answered. "I made that one just before I came here. My hip is bad. I can't get around by myself."

Several seconds ticked by as I thought about how bizarre it was that this woman would know who my grandmother was. It is a small world.

"Mrs. Ortlander," I began, "the reason I'm here is because I am tracing the family tree of Eugene Counts. Does that name mean anything to you?"

"Counts," she repeated. "Oh, Genie boy," she stated. "Yes. He and my son were great friends. Michael was very happy when he found out they were in the same platoon. It was like a miracle to actually find somebody that you knew."

"Your son died in the war?" I asked, reconfirming a fact that I already knew, and being thrilled that I had found the correct Ortlander family.

She never answered me; instead, she put her crochet work down. "In that top drawer is an album. Let me show him to you," she said. "He was my only son. I have three daughters, but he was my only son."

I did as she told me to. Never missing a beat, she went right on talking. "Genie boy was the only survivor."

"What do you mean?" I asked, skin prickling.

"Germans circled them in a valley and all were lost. It was

79

a gruesome, bloody battle. Genie boy was taken to a camp."

A Nazi POW camp. In my opinion that could change any man. It would leave him a skeleton of who he was.

"Don't know what happened to him after that. . . . I asked specifically . . ." she said.

"Asked what?"

"What happened to Michael. I wanted to know if it was a bullet or a mine. You know, did he suffer?"

"Did they tell you?"

"Walt spent many years tracking that down," she said after a pause. "We got his body way too late to view it, so we didn't know. Finally, when he found out . . . I wished I had never asked."

"What happened?" I hoped that she would tell me, even though it was a very personal question.

"His throat was cut from ear to ear," she said, and made a swooping motion that covered the entire throat.

"God, how horrible," was all I managed.

She had turned the photo album around to me, and one slender, age-spotted finger pointed out her son in his service photo. His hat was cocked to one side, he had blondish hair, and even though the photo was in black and white, I could determine that he had one blue eye and one brown eye. It was very striking.

"Why do you think Eugene survived?" I asked.

"I don't know."

"Your son was very handsome," I finally said. I didn't know what else to say to her, and she had seemed to run out of things to say to me. The awkwardness that arises when one has run out of things to say is very blatant. And embarrassing.

"I should probably be going," I said. "Thank you for your time."

Rising, I walked to the bed and touched her quilt. "It is truly magnificent," I said. "Just beautiful."

"Thank you."

She had been so peaceful when I arrived. Now there was sadness in her eyes and she worked her left hand in a nervous twitch. I wondered when the last time was that she had thought about her son's death. Had I brought up something that she had succeeded in burying? He was her only son—it would probably never be buried.

"I'm sorry, Mrs. Ortlander. About your son."

Suddenly, her face went blank and she looked at me in the oddest way. "Whatever for?" she asked.

"His suffering," I answered.

"He didn't suffer. Oh, he's not dead. I saw him once, after the war. They lied to me," she said. "They lied."

Eleven

Florence Ortlander's last words haunted me for days. I realized that she was probably in the nursing home for mental reasons and not just her hip. First the ghost story and then seeing her son supposedly alive. It was too much. I assumed it became easier for her to accept that her son had somehow lived and that she had been lied to.

Today I decided to go to my local library in New Kassel, and read through some microfilm that I had ordered. My mother's sister was the librarian there, and it had been a few weeks since I'd seen her.

I didn't take River Point Road like I normally would, because of all the sandbags. And the tourists. To have a flood is big tourism. So I went down Birne Street instead.

I turned into the parking lot and sat in the car for a minute. Something had been bugging me for several days now. It had nothing to do with Harold Zumwalt, or John Murphy, or Norah's father. It was her children.

I realize that not all children have a loving relationship with their parents. I happened to have a good relationship with my mother. And as much as my father was an old grouch and a genuine pain in the butt, I loved him just the same.

So the thing that bothered me was Rita and Jeff. Her children seemed so aloof, so removed from the horror of Norah's death. Their mother was not only dead, but murdered. They seemed saddened.

Saddened. Somehow that just didn't cut it.

I grabbed my briefcase and got out of the car. The building is small and sandy-colored, with windows that go from floor to ceiling. It houses the only microfilm reader in the entire county.

Aunt Bethany Crookshank stood behind the counter checking out a book for a little boy. She wore a pink linen jacket with an ecru blouse and skirt. The jacket brought out the pink in her cheeks and made her look remarkably young. I think some of it had to do with her state of mind. She thinks young. Younger than I do sometimes, and she is fifty-seven.

My mother is the youngest of four sisters. Emily Branham Wallace is the oldest, and owns the dairy farm out on New Kassel Outer Road. Then comes Aunt Bethany. Aunt Millicent Branham Petrovich lives in West Virginia, and then comes my mother, Jalena Branham Keith. Of the four, Aunt Bethany is probably the closest to being my soulmate. She is my companion on my many genealogical hunts, and I will be forever indebted to her for the knowledge that she bequeathed to me. And I can think of nobody I would rather traipse through a cemetery with, and that says a lot about a person.

"How are you doing?" she asked. She resembles my mother more than the other two sisters, except she is the only blond in the family. Aunt Bethany is short and trim, very classy.

"I'm all right," I said.

"Well, the microfilm reader is where it always is," she said as she pointed to the back of the room. "What are you looking for?"

"I'm not sure exactly. I'm hoping to find an obituary or announcement of some sort from the war."

"That would explain the 1942 newspapers that you ordered," she said. Aunt Bethany went about her business and I began my search through the newspapers from Partut and Ste. Genevieve Counties. The machine was one of those crank kind, and I cranked and cranked, stopping every now and then to see where I was on the film roll. I came upon some news about the war, and some bad weather. The usual things. An advertisement for women's shoes.

Those basic black pumps have come full circle.

Murdered. The word caught my attention immediately. Since discovering Norah's body I had found myself reading the gory details of the newspapers a lot more than I ever used to. In this article a young woman by the name of Gwen Geise had been murdered. I skimmed the article until I came to the method of murder. It felt like the back of my head suddenly met the front of my head.

Gwen Geise's throat had been sliced from ear to ear.

There were no other details about the murder other than the location of the body. It was an old paper and I didn't really expect there to be too many details.

The palms of my hands began to sweat. *From ear to ear.* Michael Ortlander had been murdered in the same fashion, with a slice from ear to ear. I'm sure there was more than one person in the world that killed people by slicing their throats.

But when I began to add things up, it did seem curious. I checked the date on the article. Early 1942. What if Eugene killed this woman and Michael Ortlander? But why? It was quite a coincidence that a woman from the same area as Eugene, and a friend in his platoon would be murdered in the same manner. But coincidences do happen. After all, Florence Ortlander knew who my grandmother was.

So why did this bother me so much?

I grabbed my briefcase and left the microfilm reader on. "Aunt Bethany?" I called out. "I've got to go. Sorry to rush out on you."

"No problem," I heard her say.

•

When I got home the phone was ringing off of the hook. Mother had gone to visit Grandma in Wisteria with Aunt Emily. However, Rudy was home, and I couldn't figure out why he hadn't answered it.

I grabbed the phone. "Hello?"

"Hello, Torie. It's Rita."

I was surprised to hear her voice. I couldn't think of a single reason that she would be calling, and neither could she. We spent two or three minutes in conversation without saying anything. I think she tried to pass off the phone call as a social call. You know, the just-wondering-what-you're-up-to type of call.

Well if Sheriff Brooke said anything to me for what I was about to ask her, I could always say she called me first.

"How come John Murphy didn't come to your mother's funeral?" I asked.

"Ask him," she said.

"Sheriff Brooke did ask him. He said he wasn't informed that she had died until she was already buried."

Silence hung on the other line. She was either shocked or trying to decide how to answer. What was the big deal? Why were people lying about John Murphy?

Rudy came through the kitchen then, looking perplexed. "Have you seen my watch?" he whispered.

"What?" I couldn't understand him. The whole time Rita kept talking. I gave him a dirty look, meaning to please wait.

"Jeff and I felt he had no business being there," she repeated. She thought the 'what' had been spoken to her.

"Why?" I asked.

"Where is my watch?" Rudy asked again.

"Rita, just a minute." I put my hand over the phone. "I don't know where your watch is. I don't wear it. Why should I know where it is? Or had you never thought of that novel idea?"

"Jeez," he said, and headed for the steps.

All right, don't say it. Yes, I was hateful. But I just knew Rita was ready to spill the beans. I could feel it. "Rita, thanks for holding. We had a domestic crisis. What were you saying?"

"I really don't want to get into all of this. I just wanted to call and see how the family tree was coming. I apologize, Torie, but it's really none of your business."

I hate it when people tell me that something is not any of my business. It makes me wonder *why* it's not any of my business. And then I want to know that much more what it is I'm not supposed to know.

Is nobody else inquisitive by nature?

"What if John Murphy tells me?" I asked.

"He has that right, of course."

"Where can I find him?"

"Probably at his office," she said. "He works late, all the time."

"Thanks," I said. Then we exchanged our good-byes.

I couldn't leave that lie. Before I could even get upstairs, the phone rang again. This time it was Colette, a friend of mine. Did I want to have dinner? Sure, what the heck?

•

John Murphy was in his office, just as Rita had said. It was in a modern five-story building with no real security. Most everybody had gone home; only a few lights were left on in the building, and even fewer still on the second floor, where Mr. Murphy was.

I'm not afraid of the dark, but something about hearing one's shoes clicking in a half-lit hallway . . . gives me the creeps. I felt as though I had eyes boring into my back, but every glance I gave over my shoulder assured me that I was wrong. Shivering, I tried to shake the eerie feeling, knowing that I was being ridiculous. I had probably seen too many X-Files episodes.

I knocked on the door, louder than I had intended. A slender man, about fifty-five, answered the door, barely glancing up from his papers. He was balding, and had a pen stuck behind his ear and his shirtsleeves rolled up to his elbows.

It was, of course, awkward when he finally looked up and realized he had no idea who I was.

"Who are you?" he asked.

"I'm trying to locate John Murphy."

"I'm John Murphy. Who are you? I don't take appointments this late. Call tomorrow. The office opens at nine. I'm going to have to talk to security about letting people up here."

"I saw no security."

That got his attention.

"There was nobody at the desk," I said.

He was about ready to shut the door on me when I found my

voice again. "I'm Torie O'Shea. I'm the one that found Norah's body. I had hoped that I could speak with you for a moment."

Tears welled in his eyes. "Of course. What about?"

I had the distinct feeling that he would rather discuss this somewhere else, but he led me to his desk. He sat down and motioned me to take a seat. His desk was a nice cherry wood. He had a huge swivel chair that rose way above his head in the back. Windows covered one wall, and awards of some sort covered another. No artwork, no photographs. Not even one of Norah.

He couldn't decide what to do with his hands. Strong masculine hands kept swiping at a nonexistent hair on his forehead.

"I'll be honest with you. Your name is on the top of the list of possible suspects in her death."

"Because I have no real alibi for Thursday and Friday?" he asked.

"That's one reason," I said. "But lack of alibi isn't the most damaging. I'd say the life insurance policy on Norah is the most convicting piece of information. I mean, it was supposedly to bury her with. Not only do you not bury her with it, you don't even show up at the funeral."

He looked away, and when he looked back at me, all I could see was pain. A tear ran down his face. He showed more grief than any of her children had thus far. "God," he said. A sob escaped him. "I didn't know. I didn't know. Rita and Jeff called me after it was over," he said, trying to recover himself. He rubbed his eyes. "I didn't even know she was dead," he said finally.

"Why would they do that?"

"Because Norah wanted specific things for her funeral, and her children disagreed."

"Like what?"

"Basically, *where* she wanted to be buried," he said. "She said she wanted to be buried down south. I think it was the place her mother had told her that her father was from."

"And they disagreed with that?"

"Severely. They thought it was a disgrace, that she was acting like a child over a man she'd never met."

"Had she planned on dying soon? I mean, what brought the subject up?"

He rubbed his eyes again, thinking back. "She said that the conversation came up and that she and Jeff had a huge fight over it. So she asked if I would see to everything if she provided the money for it. I said yes, and since I have no children, I asked her if she would do the same for me."

Sounded logical.

"How long were you and Norah together?" I asked.

"Years."

"Why didn't you get married?"

"She wouldn't."

"Why not live together?"

His eyes betrayed him that time. Something, I'm not sure what, lingered there in his mind.

"There were reasons."

I had stepped on sacred ground again. I can take hint. "Where were you Friday?"

"You know, I never did see any identification," he said.

"For me? Oh, I'm not a cop," I said. I laughed inwardly that he thought I was the police. I hadn't told him either way. All I had said was that I was the one that found the body. He assumed I was a cop.

"I think I've answered all the questions that I care to answer."

"Fine, but let me tell you something. I saw the worst thing of my life on that Friday. I'm not just talking about any *body*. I'm talking about a human being that I had just seen the week before, alive. And there she was, butchered. Blood everywhere, and those eyes . . . they stared right through me," I said. "It changed my life. And I suppose I've become a little obsessed about the whole thing."

I noticed he blanched slightly at my description of the scene that Friday. "I will probably never sleep again without seeing those eyes," I said. "Now, where were you Friday? You've already told the police you were out of town. Tell me where you really were or who you were with."

He paused a moment. "I was with another woman," he said

brokenly. He sobbed, and I understood why. He was with another woman when his girlfriend was killed. His guilt would consume him.

"I won't give you her name," he said.

"You don't have to unless you go to court or something," I said, unsure of the legal territory.

"I've told you this for your conscience only," he said. "To help you put it all to rest. I will deny it if the police get wind of it."

I could live with that. I stood up to help myself out the door. "I'm very sorry," I said. I was sorry that Norah was dead. I was sorry for his loss. But more than anything, I was sorry for what he would have to endure in the years to come, every time he looked in the mirror.

"Regardless of what you think, I loved her. With all my heart, I loved her."

His words rang through my ears as I walked down the half-lit halls to the elevator. That whole conversation disturbed me more than I wanted to admit. The picture it painted of Norah Zumwalt's life was bleak. She couldn't even get buried the way she wanted.

Twenty-five minutes later, I pulled into the Old Mill Stream's crowded parking lot and smiled. Colette's fancy blue sports car was parked up front. Colette was exactly what I needed after all I had been through that day.

Twelve

I had thoroughly drowned myself in a frozen jumbo margarita, and had eaten enough of those damned little chips and salsa to make me puke.

Colette was in full dress tonight. The hair was everywhere, deliberately misplaced in perfect disorder. She wore all the gold her safe-deposit box could hold, and in her hand was a cigarette which burned more than she smoked. She always reminds me of some glamour-puss from the forties, her body language being the ultimate.

She'd probably kill me if she knew that I consider her Rubenesque. She is extremely full figured, possibly even on the heavy side, but it doesn't matter. She is just as gorgeous with all of it.

We are complete opposites. I couldn't smoke a cigarette without choking to death. And I wouldn't know what to do with that much hair if I had it. But we have a long history together, being friends since fifth grade.

We talked about everything. Her in-laws, my in-laws, her new patio, and my kids. Then out of nowhere she asked me how I had been dealing with "the body."

"I suppose I'm dealing with it okay. I've been really moody. I guess I've been concentrating on why somebody would kill her instead of the fact that somebody actually killed her."

"That is just too much," she said.

"Yes," I agreed.

"I mean, shit," she said, as if that said it all. And in a way, I suppose, it did.

"Let me ask you something. Do you know anything about Zumwalt and Macklintock?" Colette knows almost everybody in St. Louis, and anybody she doesn't know, she knows somebody who does. She was born and raised in New Kassel, and when I first moved up here from Progress, she was the first person to befriend me. I fell in love with the town immediately. Colette hated it. She felt stifled. Needless to say, as soon as she graduated she went off to college in St. Louis, and she now lives in St. Louis County. She's a reporter for one of the local television stations. She isn't an anchorwoman and doesn't want to be. She likes being out on the street.

"What do you want to know?"

"I dunno," I said, shrugging.

"Best damn lawyers money can buy. I hear there is nothing they can't get done. Legal or illegal."

Great. Sheriff Brooke is messing with the Godfather. "I mean on a more personal level."

"Macklintock is gay," she said, anxious to get that piece of gossip in.

"Besides that," I said. People's sexual preference bothers me in no way. I have never experienced the homophobia that seems to plague the Midwest.

"What do you mean 'besides that'?" she asked, appalled. "It's very important when his lover works in the police department."

"Well, that could prove to be interesting. Move on. What about Zumwalt?"

Colette looked toward the ceiling, as if flipping through her mental filing cabinet. She is truly amazing in her broad scope of knowledge. She knows all the legal junk. Got a question about taxes? Insurance? Call Colette. She's extremely level-headed and calm about everything. I freak out over a parking ticket. Don't even ask how I reacted to jury duty.

Finally, she sighed. "He's sort of a weird one. The whole family was in counseling at one time."

"No kidding?" I asked. This was, in my opinion, definitely

interesting material. "How do you know this stuff?"

"I can't give out my sources. Why are you so interested? You normally don't care about St. Louis society things."

"It's driving me nuts. I want to know everything about her and why somebody would kill her."

"The snooping is my territory," she said. "Well, I don't know a whole lot about him because he never leaves the house, except to work." She thought about it a minute. "I think that there is more there than meets the eye. If you want my opinion."

"I always want your opinion."

I couldn't help but wonder if looking into this counseling bit would help me or not. It would be an intrusion, I reminded myself.

"Let's order some real food," she said with a twinkle in her eye. "What's it gonna be?"

"I can't help myself. I want the chicken fajitas." Colette always brings out the worst in me.

"Good choice. So how's your sex life?" she asked finally.

"Fine. I think Rudy is concerned about me, though. He's so cute when he's concerned about me. I don't know, maybe it reminds me that he really does love me."

"Why is he so concerned about you? 'Cause of finding the body?" she asked with a shiver.

"I think so. He's been pretty sweet about things that I think most men would have lost it over."

"Like what?"

"Just me being an all-around bitch about things. So how's your sex life?"

Asking Colette about her sex life was like asking for a four-thousand-page dissertation that read like the Kama Sutra.

She smiled. "Have I got a story for you." She settled back into her chair and prepared to tell me her story as only she could tell it.

•

After we finished our fajitas we headed for the late show. I didn't enjoy it very much because my conscience kept reminding me that I had actually eaten two dinners tonight. But about half-way through the movie I finally stopped beating myself up over it.

I arrived home at about two in the morning, wired. Movies do that to me. When I went to see *The Silence of the Lambs* with Colette, I was so wired that I talked the entire way home. She never got to say one word.

On top of it, I was broken out in hives for hours. I hate having a body that lets the entire world know when I'm upset. When I got married I had to wear a wedding dress that came up to my neck so that the hives wouldn't show.

I grabbed a Dr Pepper and headed upstairs. I sat at my desk, drinking my soda from the can. I usually get a glass, but I didn't want to make all of the noise with ice cubes and a glass.

I snooped through the box from Rita. I hadn't really looked at anything except the letters from Eugene Counts. Now it seemed I had some unspoken approval to poke through it. There were receipts, check stubs, coupons. Rita must have picked up everything on her mother's kitchen counter and thrown it in the box, too.

The quiet of the house made me settle down, and I decided I'd check through the box more thoroughly in the morning. I made my way to bed, snuggled up against Rudy, and surprisingly, was asleep in minutes.

It is not unusual for me to wake up several times in the night, even if it is just to roll over. But when I awoke at 3:46 A.M., I had a gut feeling that something was wrong.

Momentarily, I felt panicked. My eyes wouldn't focus, due to lack of sleep and the tequila. I was afraid to move. Afraid that if the boogeyman stood at the foot of my bed, he would know I was awake. Finally, I was awake enough to realize I was being ridiculous, and I sat up in bed.

It was the last calm moment of the night.

A greenish glow came from my office. Amazingly, I found the guts to get up and go see what it was. The ominous glow came from straight ahead. I knew what it was before I had a coherent thought.

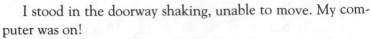

I stood in the doorway shaking, unable to move. My computer was on!

I hadn't had it on all day, so I know I didn't leave it on. Mom can't get up the steps, and my girls don't know how to turn it on. Rudy never touches the computer. Besides, he was asleep. Anyway, I don't think he would have left the foreboding message that was on the screen:

"This is a warning, Victory O'Shea. Next time will not be."

Thirteen

The chickens squawked like mad, and that scared me even more. How close had I come to catching whoever this was in the act? All I could think of was ending up like Norah.

"Rudy," I said. I ran into the bedroom and tripped over my shoes at the foot of the bed. "For God's sake, dial nine-one-one."

"I don't know where your car keys are," he mumbled.

"Rudy, wake up," I said from the floor.

"Check in the sock drawer," he said.

I got up, rubbing my shin that I had hit on the bedpost on the way down. I threw open the bedroom window in time to get a glance of a dark figure jumping onto our wheelbarrow and then over the fence and into the woods. "Don't bother calling nine-one-one," I said as I looked down at him. He hadn't budged. I could be dead for all he cared. "Rudy, wake up!" I yelled. I gave the foot of the bed a good swift kick.

"What the hell?" he asked. He came to, throwing the covers off. The more he tried to get the covers off, the more tangled he became.

"Call Sheriff Brooke," I said.

I took the steps two at a time. The first floor met my feet with a thud in nothing flat. I gripped the banister as I turned down the hall.

"Mom? Everybody okay down here?"

"I think so," she said. It was not surprising that she didn't seem as though she'd been asleep.

"Be right back," I said to her. I went to the bedroom opposite hers and was very relieved to see that Mary and Rachel had not awoken. Rachel scratched her belly, mumbled something, and rolled over. Mary never moved. She just lay, spread-eagled on her back, with her mouth open and snoring.

I went back to Mom's room. "Somebody was in my office."

"I know," she said. "You know how light I sleep. I heard whoever it was come in the window, but I couldn't do anything. There was no way to warn you without letting whoever it was know that I was awake."

"Well, we'll fix that. You're getting your own private phone line installed this week."

"Torie?" Rudy called from upstairs.

"I'll be back, Mom."

I didn't want this making the local news, I thought as I headed back up the steps. I thought it would be best if I didn't panic and run like a fraidycat. Isn't that exactly what the person wanted? He wanted to scare me. If he had wanted to kill me, he would have. Or he would wait until he got me alone; he wouldn't warn me first.

Within fifteen minutes Sheriff Brooke arrived, disheveled and concerned. He was also slightly irritated. There must have been something in my face that told him the seriousness of the matter, because as soon as he came in the house and got a good look at me, the irritation disappeared.

Briefly I told him what had happened, and of course he wanted to see the computer. We went upstairs, both windows open now, letting in a nice June breeze.

"Did you touch it?" he asked.

"No. Not since yesterday anyway."

"Let me get somebody in here to get some prints," he said, reaching for the phone.

"I don't really think the guy would leave his prints all over the keyboard," I said.

Sheriff Brooke shoved his hands on his hips and glared at me. "Let me do my job."

"I just don't want this person to know how much he scared me."

"So you want to be dead instead?" he asked me. "What did you do today that might have caused this?" he asked.

"I was about to ask you the same thing," I said, angry at his accusation, however warranted. My hair resembled a short version of the Bride of Frankenstein's, and I wore an oversize T-shirt with stains of every color and size on it, big fuzzy house slippers, and a scowl. I was in no mood to be jerked around.

"Torie, let the sheriff do his job," Rudy said. He was trying to be in control of the situation. It was difficult for him to do when he was standing in his Santa underwear. They weren't just any Santa underwear. Santa was in his swimming trunks sitting under a palm tree. My mother bought those for him for Christmas one year.

He must have read my mind because he glanced down at the front of himself. He grabbed his robe from the floor and said, "I'll be in the john."

"I confronted Zumwalt with my theory," Sheriff Brooke said to me. Then he said into the phone, "This is Brooke. I'm at forty-one twenty-six River Point Road in New Kassel. Send over a unit. There's been a break-in." He hung up the phone.

"What theory?" I asked, dumbfounded.

"That he killed his ex-wife for the insurance money," he said. A smile lingered on his face. The confrontation must have been a sight to behold. I wish I could have been there.

"Really? You said that?" I asked, impressed as hell.

Somehow I got the impression that Sheriff Brooke didn't have any real suspects. I think he was just trying to stir up all of the hornets' nests, hoping the right hornet would fly out at him.

"Not in those exact words," he said. "But he got the picture. He started to twitch and sweat, and now . . . you have a break-in," he said as he crossed his arms and leaned up against my bookshelves. Which, by the way, cover two walls of my office.

"Did you mention my name?" I asked.

"No, but Jeff and Rita probably have." He was silent, waiting for my confession.

"All I did was go and visit Michael Ortlander's mother. You know, the friend of Eugene's."

"What?!" he yelled, nearly knocking my precious leather copy of *The Bostonians* off of the shelf. "Damn it!" he yelled at nobody in particular. He paced back and forth and ran his fingers through his hair.

"I thought—," he began loudly, then stopped himself and counted to ten. He showed considerable restraint when riled, I noticed admiringly. "I thought we were going to go together," he said.

"If we went to see Eugene Counts," I said defiantly. "I didn't go to see Eugene Counts."

He burned slowly for a few seconds. "I'm going to throw your butt in jail," he said, pointing his finger at me.

So much for restraint.

"Did you forget already what Norah looked like? Did you forget the blood?" he asked. "I cannot believe you would be so stupid."

"Nothing happened. The little old lady told me how her son died and Counts was the only survivor of the whole platoon. He went to a POW camp."

"So?"

"So unless Florence Ortlander has a set of bionic legs, or Doris the bedpan-wielding nurse from hell jumped out my window, you're barking up the wrong tree," I said. I was getting louder by the minute. "Nobody else knew I was there," I added as my closing argument.

He waited silently, as if he knew there was more to the story. And waited. And I began to feel really guilty, so I just said it.

"Of course, I did go to see John Murphy last night, too."

Sheriff Brooke sat down on that one, putting his head in his hands. He looked as if he were going to explode or cry, I wasn't sure which, and figured this was no time to point out the fact that he was sitting on my stack of *Books in Print*. Aunt Bethany always makes sure that I get the old set when the new ones come in at the library.

"You didn't say anything about staying away from John Murphy."

"And what did you learn?"

"I don't think he did it."

"Why not?" he asked snottily. "Please, pray tell."

"Because he cried."

"He cried."

"It was the way he cried. I guess you just had to be there," I said.

"Which I wasn't," he reminded me.

"Don't look at me like that. He's got an alibi. He was with another woman," I said.

"And until he names her, and she's questioned, he remains without an alibi," he informed me. I love learning all of this police stuff.

"The insurance policies were legitimate," I said.

"How did you know about the insurance . . . ? Forget it. What makes you so sure about the insurance policies?" he asked.

"Rita didn't want to discuss why they hadn't told John about Norah's death. That leads me to believe that John's story is correct."

"I bet if you talk to Jeff or Rita, you'll hear just the opposite," he said.

"Possibly."

"I'm going to tell Newsome to be more careful about where he's at when he's discussing investigations."

It won't do any good, I thought. I'm nosy by nature.

Fourteen

I truly believe that Sheriff Colin Brooke was beginning to wish he had never met me. I didn't care.

There was no way that I was going to leave this alone, and Brooke knew it. The break-in and the message that was left on my computer had answered one vital question.

There was no way that Norah Zumwalt's murder could have been a random act of violence. It was somebody who knew her.

It was almost noon, just about nine hours after the invasion of my home. Rudy had been much more affected by this than I had first thought. He called three different security-system companies by nine o'clock. Our security system would be installed within the week.

I began looking through the contents of Norah Zumwalt's box with much deliberation. Every piece of paper I examined closely.

Rudy came upstairs, never looked at me, and went straight to the bedroom. I noticed, but said nothing. I flipped off the radio that had been playing a piano sonata. I had recognized the piece but not well enough to name it.

Telephone bills, electric bills, and a parking ticket were among the items in the box that Rita gave me. Two things in particular struck me. There was a call on her phone bill to a number in Vitzland, Missouri. What a coincidence—the same town that Eugene Counts lived in. But the call was made days before she came to my office at the historical society. Could she have just called all the E. Countses in various directories, try-ing to find him? The call was under a minute, as if she hung up as soon as she heard his voice.

The second thing that bothered me . . . Just then Rudy threw his suitcase on the bed.

"Honey, do you have a business trip this week?" I asked.

Silence. The second thing that bothered me was the paper-work from the veterinarian. According to the papers in my hand, Norah's dog was scheduled to be in the vet's office at eleven o'clock the morning she died. Rita had said that Jeff took the dog in to get its shots. So how did the paperwork end up at the house if Jeff saw her last on Thursday? Maybe he brought it to Rita later and she just threw it in the box with her mother's other things.

Would you mess with a receipt from a veterinarian if your mother had been murdered? I wouldn't. This didn't sit well with me.

Rudy threw his pants at the suitcase, missing it by a mile. I could see the bed from my office but nothing else. I stepped to the doorway, reading another piece of paper. All it said was: "Cora Landing. 5:30 Thursday."

"Rudy, is something wrong?"

Silence.

"Look, if you don't tell me what's wrong, how can I argue with you?"

"I don't want to argue with you," he said without looking at me. "I want you to use your head."

"What?"

"You're one of the most intelligent human beings I've ever met, Torie. Use that brain of yours. You've got to stop. Norah has become an obsession. This is our home, Torie. Our children live here. Your mother lives here. I don't like what's happening."

"Do you think I invited somebody to break into our home?" I asked.

"No, but you're ticking somebody off. You're not a cop, you're not a PI, so why don't you act like the good little tour guide that you are and leave this to the sheriff?"

I could get really ticked off here, I thought. But I breathed deeply and pretended to be happy. "Are you going somewhere?"

"Chicago," he said. "Be back in two days. Do you see what I mean? This trip has been on the calendar for a month, and you're so far out in the ozone that you completely forgot about it. I'm afraid to leave you alone."

"Are you suggesting that you are my baby-sitter?"

"You need one," he said angrily.

Okay, I was ticked now.

"I don't understand, Rudy. What's the problem here? Is it the break-in, or are you just jealous because I've had some excitement in my life the last few months? I wish I had never found Norah's body, but I did. I wish I could have just stayed ignorant of everything and played with the old ladies at the historical society all summer. But I did find her. And now I have a chance to do something about it. I didn't think I could at first, but now I think I can really help Sheriff Brooke."

"Finding her murderer is not more important than your family's safety," he said.

"I realize that," I said. "But we're getting an alarm, and I don't think that this person will hurt us. It would be stupid."

"Killing Norah was stupid."

He chewed on the inside of his lip, and his brown eyes turned soft. "I can't be here all the time," he said. "I don't want to come home from a business trip and have Sheriff Brooke meet me at the door telling me you're dead."

I reached up and brushed my fingers across his eyebrow. He was genuinely concerned for me. Rudy usually treats me as though I can take care of myself most of the time. He was showing macho pigheaded concern. And I actually sort of liked it. He pulled me to him and kissed me. I kissed him back with passion. He knocked the suitcase on the floor and we landed on the bed.

"I'll be careful. Besides, Sheriff Brooke doesn't think he'll attempt this again. He's made his point," I said as he kissed me on the neck.

"And if the sheriff is wrong?" he asked me. His breath was warm on my ear.

"Shush," I said, and kissed him.

•

Two hours later I stood in my office at the Gaheimer House freaking out over the fact that the New Kassel Museum would open in three days.

"Are all of the donations taken care of?" Sylvia asked.

"Everything except the Prussian vase that Tobias Thorley is donating. He said that his grandfather brought it with him when he came over."

We had been taking donations for the museum, in the form of money or items. Sylvia had even forked over a few of the items from the Gaheimer House. Elaine Dinwiddie, Staci and Elmer Kolbe, and myself had worked long and hard on displays. I got to write the blurbs for all of the items, checked over by Sylvia Pershing, of course.

But we were down to the wire and I didn't have any food or music lined up for the weekend's festivities, and Sylvia wanted much more than Tobias's accordion wonders.

There was a knock on the door. I looked up and there was Sheriff Brooke.

"Hiya, Torie."

"Hello, Sheriff. Please come in."

Sylvia made no attempt to leave; instead, she nearly growled at him as he nodded acknowledgment to her.

"Sylvia," I said. "This is Sheriff Brooke."

"I'm well aware of who he is," she said.

"Well I thought so. He's been our sheriff for a while, but you never speak to him when you see him. I assumed you didn't know who he was."

I would probably pay dearly for that little dig.

"Oh, yes," Sheriff Brooke said. "We know each other quite well. This is my aunt, sort of."

I'm glad there were no flies in the office because I would have assuredly caught one in my open mouth. I felt myself sit down, not paying the least bit of attention to whether the chair was behind me or not.

"Explain," I said.

"Well, my grandmother's first husband was Sylvia's brother. My father being born to my grandmother's second husband. So, I'm not sure what that makes us," he said.

"It makes us nothing!" she said. "My brother got what he deserved for lusting."

"It makes Sylvia your great step-aunt, if there is such a thing," I said.

"Torie, I will not allow this sort of behavior from one of my staff. I want upstanding role models of the community. I shall have to replace you with Mary Emma Wiggs if you keep consorting with . . . him."

"Mary Emma Wiggs is a good woman. If you feel the need to replace me, then by all means, do."

We had a staring contest, Sylvia and I. And for the first time in history, I actually won. She stormed out of the office with all the regality of a queen, not so much as glancing in Sheriff Brooke's direction.

"I'm sorry," I said to the sheriff after she had left.

"Don't worry about it. I thought you handled her pretty well."

"If I could only figure out what makes her like that, I could probably handle her even better."

"Good luck. So, are you ready?"

"For what?"

"I thought you might like to pay Mr. Eugene Counts a visit."

I wasn't sure why he asked me to go, unless it was because I knew a great deal about Eugene Counts and his family. Maybe he just wanted to get my opinion of Eugene Counts. I started to say yes, and then remembered the museum and a very upset Sylvia Pershing. But when would I ever get a chance like this again?

In the car, I learned a lot. Sheriff Brooke was much more talkative today than in the past. Maybe it was because I was more receptive. I have a way of finding out things about people, when I'm in the right kind of mood. People just open up and talk to me.

I found out that he was forty-two in March. Divorced twice, with three children. He had been valedictorian of Wisteria High School in 1971. Culinary school followed before he decided on a career in law enforcement.

Not at all what I had expected. I had figured that Sheriff Brooke was the type to eat cold pizza and beer for breakfast and would have to smell his socks to see if they were the clean ones.

I filled him in on a more detailed account of the conversation that I had had with Mrs. Ortlander. I had called both Rita and Jeff earlier to see if they knew of a Cora Landing. I wasn't even sure if it was a who or a what. The sheriff had no idea who she was, but he would check it out.

"Did you check out the calls on Norah's long-distance bill?" I asked.

"Yes."

"What about the call to Vitzland?" I asked.

I could see the lightbulb go on over his head. "Newsome said that everything checked out. There were two calls that were under a minute. They were wrong numbers."

"It's Eugene Counts. I called it from the office this afternoon and a woman answered and said 'Counts residence.' Not that I really thought it was anybody else. I knew it had to be him."

He shook his head. "We didn't know who Eugene Counts was at the time."

"Of course, it makes perfect sense that he would have thought it was a wrong number," I said.

Vitzland was a town without a McDonald's or any other fast-food joint. It was a small town with two gas stations, a Big J grocery store, and a school. One could get to Vitzland by taking River Point Road or Hermann Avenue out of New Kassel and heading south about ten or fifteen miles. It sat right across the border of Granite County; therefore, all calls were long distance.

Sheriff Brooke pulled into a gas station and asked for directions, which I found to be a very uncommon characteristic for a man. Most men will drive around in circles with the sun setting several times on them before asking for directions. I suppose somewhere in their code of honor it is written: "Thou shalt not ask for directions, lest you be thought of as incompetent."

Within two minutes we were sitting in front of Eugene Counts's home, and I was petrified. What if he was the person that broke into my home? A lot of seventy-year-old people are in good enough condition to climb a ladder and jump a fence. He could be a Jane Fonda workout freak. But he had no reason to know who I was, I reminded myself.

Sheriff Brooke sensed my nervousness. "You're fine," he said.

All I could think of was Eugene's innocent face, his dark eyes and features perfectly poised under his army hat. If he had murdered the girl in the newspaper article and his friend Michael Ortlander, then the killings were done *before* his internment at the POW camp. Which meant the camp hadn't changed him. He was what he was, and he had everybody fooled.

"I just got a bad feeling, you know?" I asked.

"I know all about those," he said.

Eugene Counts owned a large farmhouse on a street with several other large homes that resembled the farmhouse style. It had a huge porch with a glider sitting on it. I tried to imagine him sitting there on his glider, looking out at the neighborhood. Was he at peace when he did that? Or was he thinking back to the murders, savoring every detail like the sick puppy I thought him to be?

Did his neighbors suspect? Were they oblivious? Could these deviants of society really exist right alongside everybody else? I wasn't sure I wanted to know the answers to the questions that plagued me in those last few seconds before Sheriff Brooke rang the doorbell.

I was glad we were on the porch because it was raining again. Some levees had already burst. So far, the New Kassel one was holding its own. We waited for what seemed like an eternity before anybody answered the door, and I felt my stomach drop to my toes. There was no turning back now. I was here.

A woman answered. It was obvious that she was the cleaning lady or some other sort of domestic employee. She was in jeans and a shirt, but the white nurse's shoes and apron gave it away.

The voice was quiet as she managed a "Hello."

"Yes, is Mr. Counts in today?"

"Who are you?"

"Sheriff Colin Brooke, Granite County," he said, badge flashing.

She didn't seem shocked or worried. She just excused herself and closed the door, leaving us to stand on the porch. Sheriff Brooke looked around the neighborhood, seeing things through a policeman's eyes. There was no way I could see the same things.

The door opened, and she ushered us in and left. The pit of my stomach turned with every grueling second that she was gone. This was Norah's father. In March, if somebody would have told me that I would be standing in the living room of the father of Norah Zumwalt, I would've laughed.

"What are you going to say?" I asked Brooke. "Hello, why did you kill the daughter you never knew existed?"

"Shh," he said.

A tall and stately man appeared. I knew he was supposed to be seventy years old, but he came across a decade younger.

"Yeah?" he asked.

If the woman who answered the door had told him that we were the police or with the sheriff, he gave no hint of it. He treated us with the calm but slightly irritated tolerance that one would give a shoe salesman.

"Mr. Counts, I'm Sheriff Colin Brooke, with the Wisteria Police Department." Brooke was so professional when he flashed his badge.

Eugene Counts never said a word. He was dressed in a pink golf shirt and wild printed pants. He was dressed for the golf course, but the rain would not likely let up.

"Your telephone number showed up on the records of a woman who was murdered a couple of months ago," he said, watching for any sort of reaction. "It could have been a wrong number, but we thought if you were acquainted with her, you might give us some clue as to why she was murdered."

"What was the name?" he asked, not moving a single muscle except to speak. His reserve was remarkable, and he still had not stepped completely into the living room.

I glanced around, hoping to see some clue to his past life, his former self. I found no such thing. His living room was cozy, but impersonal. No photographs or plaques graced the walls or the tables. There was absolutely nothing to give a hint as to who its owner was. Not even a clue that the man was a veteran. I had an eerie feeling that the entire house would be like that.

"The woman's name was Norah Zumwalt," the sheriff said.

Again, to my great disappointment, the name of his daughter brought no reaction from him. He only thought a moment and said, "I suppose it was a wrong number. I don't know anybody by that name."

"You're sure?" Sheriff Brooke asked.

"Yes," he said.

There was something about him suddenly that didn't sit right. Hands in his pockets, he waited for more. The woman came back into the living room, whether by accident or curiosity, I couldn't be certain. Eugene gave her one glance, and she went as fast as she could back in the other direction. He never said a word, just glanced. That glance had been powerful enough to send the woman scurrying like some sort of street rat.

I wanted to scream at him. I wanted to know—no, I wanted to *demand* why he had abandoned his mother? Why had he abandoned the woman, Viola, to whom he had expressed his undying love? Was it all a game? Was none of it real to him? It was certainly real to Edith Counts. To Viola Pritcher.

"Well, I'm sorry to have bothered you. If it would come up, can you vouch for your whereabouts on May second of this year?" the sheriff asked him.

"If it should come up," he answered, "you can ask my lawyer."

He was smooth. I was irate with Sheriff Brooke. I could barely believe my ears. Why had we driven down here to ask him one question? We could have done that on the phone! I was furious, and believe me, Sheriff Brooke was going to hear about it.

"Gene," a male voice from down the hall said.

"Be right there," he answered.

"Like I said," Sheriff Brooke began. "Sorry to have bothered you."

"Excuse me," I said, and swallowed. I was scared to death, but if I didn't ask him this question, I would never forgive myself. "I'd like to ask you a question. I'd like to ask you about the death of Michael Ortlander."

A pale gray ring formed around his mouth as the color drained from his face. It was much like watching a cartoon. I had no idea that a simple question like that would have received such a reaction. Of course, Sheriff Brooke had the same pale look to him, too, but I knew it wasn't for the same reason.

"Get out," Counts said in a steely, cold voice.

"He was your friend, wasn't he? His mother is very interested in the circumstances concerning his death."

I had him going now. He probably couldn't figure for the life of him how we went from a wrong number to knowing about Michael Ortlander! And I reveled in my superior intelligence, for the moment.

Sheriff Brooke, on the other hand, had a look about him which suggested that, for the first time in his life, he was contemplating murder. Either that or he had just seen his career and his pension fly right out the window.

Eugene moved toward us very quickly, shaking from fear or anger. I hoped it wasn't anger because I suspected what he did to his so-called friends. I could just imagine what he did to his enemies. He opened the door to let us out. I turned a foot away from him on the porch, facing him and all of his deceit.

"I'm sorry," I said, trying to appease him. "I thought he was your friend. I spoke with his mother—"

I did not finish my sentence.

I could not physically finish my sentence. At that moment, something clicked, and I was stunned into silence. That was probably the first time that phenomenon had ever happened to me.

Eugene stared at me with one brown eye and one blue eye. This man was not Eugene Counts. Eugene had the dark brown eyes and unsettling good looks of a French rogue. The man who stared at me with hatred was Michael V. Ortlander!

"Don't ever come back here," he said, and shut the door.

•

Sheriff Brooke dragged me from the porch. My discovery of Counts's real identity had astonished me so much that I couldn't find the muscles to make my legs work. Unusual things were happening to my reflexes these days, and I didn't like it. It was as if I were a puppet, and somebody else was controlling what I did. The ordinary reactions that once upon a time I could have counted on were failing.

Once we were in the car and on the two-lane blacktop road, Sheriff Brooke let me have it.

"What the hell was that all about?" His nostrils flared, and I could sense that he was trying very hard to control himself.

"Florence Ortlander wasn't crazy," I managed.

"You had no business—"

"I can't believe it."

"—asking him a question like that."

"It was there the whole time."

"What are you? Nuts?"

"I just couldn't see it. If I had looked from the right point of view, maybe."

"That's it, you're nuts."

"Mom probably saw it. She sees everything."

"You're nuts, and I'm dead," he said.

It was quiet a few minutes. Each one of us tried to take in the situation at hand and sighed with relief that we had just survived the previous situation unscathed.

"What did you say?" Brooke asked.

"Florence Ortlander, she wasn't crazy. She said that she saw her son alive after the war. I didn't tell you that part of the conversation because I just thought it was the ramblings of a senile old woman. I thought she was crazy. But she probably did see him."

Sheriff Brooke beat the steering wheel with the palm of his hand. Then he breathed deeply. "Do you know why I asked you to come along today?"

"Why?"

"Because you see things totally different than I do. Maybe it's because you're not a cop. Maybe it's because I need a vacation. Whatever the reason, the only leads that I have in this case are because of you."

That took a lot for him to say, I grant you. I watched him mutely as the road led us into a valley of grazing horses.

"But," he said, "you can't just pull that kind of . . . stuff."

"Florence was convinced that her son had somehow survived the war," I began. "She claimed that she saw him one day, long after the war had ended. Evidently, he didn't see her, or he pretended not to see her," I said. "All of this time, she was right, and nobody believed her, I bet."

"Come again?" he said.

"That wasn't Eugene Counts back there. That was Michael Ortlander."

"What? But how . . . ?"

"That man had one blue eye and one brown eye. Eugene had deep dark brown eyes. Once I made the connection, it was easy to see that he was the same man that Florence showed me as being her son. Just older," I said. My heart pumped, and my blood pressure was about to come out the top of my head. "I'd say he killed Eugene Counts and swapped dog tags with him. He went to a POW camp as the sole survivor of his platoon, so nobody would ever be the wiser. Except Eugene's girlfriend and family couldn't figure out why he never contacted them. He also hadn't banked on Eugene, the real Eugene, having fathered a child."

"But why would Ortlander kill Eugene Counts?" Sheriff Brooke asked.

"I think he killed that girl back in the forties," I said. The sheriff looked lost. "Did I tell you about her? Well, anyway, the wound was identical to Eugene's. So if the police ever got too close to catching her killer, Ortlander didn't have to worry, because he was no longer Ortlander! He was a new person. He was now Eugene Counts," I said with a sweeping motion of my hands.

I noticed Sheriff Brooke had pulled off of the two-lane road and turned into a gas station. Low and behold, an attendant, yes, a real breathing human being, asked Sheriff Brooke how much gas he needed, just as the sheriff was taking off his seat belt to get out. Sheriff Brooke looked as shocked as I felt at the attendant's arrival.

"Ten dollars, regular. Is there anyplace to get some food around here?" he asked.

Red hair and freckles were all I could see for all the grease on the attendant. "Big J grocery."

"No, I mean, like a restaurant?"

"Nope. You headed north?" Sheriff Brooke nodded in agreement. "Closest place is about ten or fifteen miles up the road at New Kassel," he answered.

"Guess we'll just wait until we get home," the sheriff said. He never looked at me as he asked the inevitable. "You think Ortlander killed Norah because she found out he wasn't Eugene Counts?"

However relieved I was that Eugene Counts was not a mass murderer, it was still difficult for me to switch the identities. I had come to think of Eugene Counts as alive and breathing in Vitzland, Missouri. Now I had to think of him as having died in Europe during the war.

"I think it's a real good possibility," I said. "But Norah Zumwalt never let on that she knew he was alive."

It was hard to say what Sheriff Brooke was thinking. Hell, I'd just handed him a fifty-year-old murder to solve, as well. I wouldn't be surprised if he didn't enlist my help anymore. After all, I seemed to create work for him.

"What about the neighbors? You get all their statements?" I asked.

"Yup. Nobody saw or heard nothing. How can a woman be stabbed repeatedly and not be heard?"

I just shook my head. How come nobody knew about John Murphy? How come there was no murder weapon? No motive? No motive, until now.

"The only thing we have even close to a clue from the neighbors is a car that was parked in front of her house on Thursday night. It wasn't Rita's or Jeff's."

"That could have been the person that came to her door when I called her."

"Yup."

"What kind of car?"

"An aqua-colored Toyota."

He was smiling. "What?" I asked, trying to get him to let me in on his secret.

"There was an aqua-colored Toyota parked across the street from Eug—Michael Ortlander's house."

"What?" I asked, flabbergasted. "Was it Ortlander's?"

"Don't think so. Ortlander's car was in the driveway, maybe even one in the garage."

"So why are you smiling?" I asked.

"Because it could have been somebody visiting Ortlander."

Of course. The male voice I had heard from the hallway when the sheriff and I were in the living room. "Well, did you—"

"Got the license plate number," he said with a broad smile as he paid the attendant and pulled out of the gas station. He then headed up Hermann Avenue to New Kassel.

•

When I finally got home, there was a message on the phone table in the foyer for me to call John Murphy. What could he possibly want with me? Had I given him my phone number? I was still pretty shaken from earlier and wasn't sure that I wanted to talk with anybody. Still, it pricked my conscience until I called him back. He answered, sounding tired and depressed.

"This is Murphy."

"Hi, this is Victory O'Shea."

"Mrs. O'Shea, I'm glad that you called. I don't know how to say this, but what would you like for me to do with this money?"

"What money?"

"The money from Norah's . . . policy. I can't keep it."

Why was he asking me? But then again, who else would he ask? Jeff and Rita? I couldn't think of an appropriate person for him to give it to. "I don't know. How about giving it to a charity that she was fond of?"

"Yeah, maybe. I might give it to the symphony or something."

"She also has an aunt that lives in Washington, Missouri. She could probably use it." The memory of Louise Shenk came to me. Her house was modest and comfortable. But it was her labored breathing that I thought of. The woman's health was not the greatest. That money might come in handy for medical reasons. Besides, Norah probably would have left her something, if she had known about her. "Her name is Louise Shenk, and now that I think about it, I think that would be your best bet."

"Do you have an address?"

"Yes." He was quiet on the other end. "Is there something else on your mind?"

"Yes. I want to somehow explain myself."

"There is no need. You don't owe me anything."

"Yes, I do. Besides, I need to say this." He sighed heavily and jumped in. "I was having an affair because I felt my relationship with Norah was a dead end. It was going nowhere, and I needed more."

I always wonder what is going on in a person's head when he is in the middle of a confession. Was he telling me everything that he felt? Or was he telling me a very carefully thought-out confession, omitting certain details, adding other? I can remember confessing to going to a carnival once when I was a teenager and had been told I couldn't go. But I very carefully left out the part about the boy that I went with. It was a confession, but a very limited confession. I wondered if this is what I was getting from John Murphy.

"I loved Norah too much to let her go completely," he said. "She wouldn't marry me because her first marriage caused her too much grief. The reason she wouldn't live with me was because of her children."

Believe it or not, I could understand that logic. I didn't necessarily agree with it, but I could understand it.

"Her life was not her own, Mrs. O'Shea. You'll never know. Not one minute of her life was ever her own."

He didn't say good-bye; he just hung up, leaving me with a sadness. I didn't agree with his affair. Although they weren't married, there must have been some sort of verbal agreement between them, of their loyalties, or he wouldn't have felt so guilty about his affair. But I couldn't point fingers at him quite as easily as I normally would have.

Fifteen

Water finally claimed the Old Mill Stream. It sat between the Mississippi River and Kassel Creek, and the water was even too much for the sandbags. It was the only place in town that had flooded so far. I was in the second floor of the Old Mill Stream helping the mayor and his wife carry out dining chairs and tables, along with china and linens. I could not believe that I had had dinner there with Colette just a week before.

"Did you see that farmhouse on television this morning?" Zella Castlereagh asked me.

"Yes," I said. "I can't believe a house stood for ninety years, and the water just took it away." I flashed back in my mind to that morning, when I was watching the television. A levee broke in Illinois and washed away a two-story farmhouse as if it were made out of Popsicle sticks. I cried. I think everybody within two states cried.

Zella is a kind woman. She has sparkling blue eyes with auburn hair, now turned slightly gray. I never could figure out why she married Bill. Our mayor is primarily concerned with monetary things. Zella is the furthest thing from that. They bought the Old Mill Stream about twenty years ago, and it was one of my favorite places to eat.

"The house didn't bother me so much," Bill said. "It was the dead bodies."

Yes the dead bodies were enough to send a chill down H. P. Lovecraft's spine. The water had not only destroyed crops and people's property; it had flooded cemeteries as well. Dead bodies were floating in the floodwaters of west-central Missouri. Empty caskets floated down the river. I would rather bullfight in a closet than have to round up those bodies and identify them. I thanked God that I didn't have to.

"I agree, Bill," I said. "The bodies were . . . indescribable."

Bill and I carried a table down the steps. I volunteered to go down backward, since I was a good thirty years younger than he was. Elmer Kolbe and Chuck Velasco were downstairs taking out paintings and other valuables that were not affected by the water. There was about a foot and a half of water on the main level. We were taking things out in case the water got any higher.

My foot hit the water with a splash. I had worn thongs so that I could just toss them in the trash when this was over. Floodwater is disgusting. It felt like little "things" were nibbling at my ankles. God only knew what was in the water. I'm sure the "nibbling" was my overactive imagination.

It was still early in the day. I had started helping the Castlereaghs around eight in the morning. I was getting hungry.

Bill guided me out the front door and we put the table in the parking lot, along with everything else we had taken out of the mill so far. He was going to store as much of it as he could in Wisteria at the U-Store.

"Well, Bill. I'm hungry. If you don't mind, I'm going to head on home, get a shower, and eat some lunch," I said.

"That's fine, Torie," he said. The sweat gleamed off of his bald head. "We really appreciate the help."

"No problem. I'll be back some time later today."

I arrived home, aggravated, hot, and madder than a hornet. My anger could only be directed at Mother Nature. As I stepped up onto my front porch, I turned and looked back out over the swollen Mississippi. I had such a great view because I was on a hill. I couldn't for the life of me figure out where all of the water would go once this was all over. Where does it all go?

I wiped at a tear I hadn't even realized I had shed.

Once I was inside, the house was quiet. Mom was on the back porch painting. The kids were in the yard playing on the swing set.

Elk graced the canvas in front of Mom, along with a mountain peak and a forest of trees.

"Looks good," I said as I kissed her on top of her head.

"Thanks," she said. "Your dad called yesterday while you were out with Sheriff Brooke."

"Really?" I asked. I hadn't heard from him in a while and was thinking about calling him. "What did he want?"

"Wanted to know if he could borrow your house."

"What for?"

"Jam session," she said. She put gold highlights on her trees with a small round brush.

"Jam session?" My dad is a musician from the early sixties, and although he hasn't played for money in twenty years, he and his buddies like to get together once in a while. It's great fun, and I encourage anyone who has never sat in on a jam session to do so. Especially if the people jamming are old farts who like to add a blues touch to songs like "Red Red Wine."

Dad's house is in the city and he can't do it there because everybody calls the police on him.

"Sure, I don't care," I said. "As a matter of fact, I'll barbecue for all of them."

I was up to listening to some George Jones and Patsy Cline. I love all music.

Mom said nothing as she added a stroke to her painting. When she was finished with that particular tree branch, she said, "How come Sheriff Brooke took you to see Eugene Counts?" Her tongue went to her upper lip. Somehow, her tongue made her paint better.

"I'm not sure. He says it's because I see things differently than he does. You know, a different angle," I said as the cat rubbed my leg.

"I agree with that. Your angle is completely different than his, and it just may be the angle he needs to solve the case."

"Oh," I said.

"I think Sheriff Brooke is very relieved to have stumbled on you in this case. 'Course, he probably rues the day at the same time," she said. "You have that effect upon people."

I wasn't insulted. It was the truth. Why get all bent out of shape over something that's so obviously the truth? "I must get that from my father's side of the family."

She smiled. "So, how was your visit with Eugene Counts?"

"Turned out to be Michael Ortlander."

"Figured as much."

"What?" I screamed. "What do you mean you figured as much? Are you saying that you knew Eugene Counts was really Michael Ortlander all along? I find that hard to believe."

"Well, not that specifically. But I knew something wasn't right. And as soon as you said it, it seemed to make perfect sense."

"Well move over, Miss Marple," I said.

Mom was genuinely surprised at my irritation with her. But before she could give me a rebuttal, the phone rang.

I hurried into the kitchen from the porch, expecting the call to be from either Rudy or Sheriff Brooke. I was wrong.

"Mrs. O'Shea?" a voice asked.

"This is she."

"Hope I'm not disturbing you. This is Harold Zumwalt." Somebody could have driven a dump truck through my mouth. It was certainly open wide enough.

"Norah's ex-husband . . ."

"I know who you are," I said. "What do you want?" My heart rate doubled, and I tried to sound as normal as I could. I failed miserably.

"I was wondering if I could speak with you," he said as if this were the most normal of invitations.

"Why me? Why don't you call Sheriff Brooke?" I asked.

"Because you found her. Please, I just want to talk. Can you come to my home? I don't eat in public places."

"Let me get this straight. You're inviting me to lunch?"

I know, I should have said no. But it was so tempting. I found myself asking for directions. As soon as I had agreed to meet him, I felt funny about it. After all, I really knew nothing about him. What did I really know about any of them? But I'd already told him yes, and I was going.

I took a quick shower, threw on a pair of light cotton dress pants and a shirt, and my brown sandals. Putting on some blush and mascara, I tried to think of what I'd say to him. Should I ask him about the family's therapy sessions? Maybe he'd bring that up on his own. It was doubtful, but I couldn't think of what he wanted to talk to me about.

I brushed my teeth and grabbed my purse, pausing at the stairs. What if he was the person who broke into my house? Maybe he wanted to kill me and shove me down the garbage disposal. Who would ever know?

Finding a piece of paper, I wrote in big black marker: "Went to Harold Zumwalt's. If not back by 5:00, call Brooke."

Taping it on the screen of my computer, I grabbed my letter opener at the same time and shoved it in my purse. Just in case. I don't own a gun and don't want to. But one would have sure come in handy right about then. No it wouldn't, I told myself. I'd probably shoot myself in the foot. I really wasn't worried for my safety. If I had been truly concerned about it, I wouldn't have gone.

All I told my mother was that I'd be back by five. I kissed the girls and headed out to the car. I was on northbound Highway 55 in no time, waiting anxiously for the exit to 270 West, so that I could find my way to Ladue.

I arrived at his house, completely unprepared for what I saw. His house would sell for a couple of million on the market. This wasn't a house, it was an estate. The grounds were surrounded by a stone fence, and contained many large trees. Wonder what it would be like to have *grounds* instead of a yard. The gate that I passed through even had an attendant on duty.

The house was a massive white structure with pillars in the front, reminding me of what the library at Alexandria would have looked like. Tennis courts were in the back; I caught a peek as I drove up. He had a stable and all sorts of outer buildings that he had to hunt for reasons to use. He probably hired somebody to think of reasons to use things. What would his position be called anyway?

I had no idea where to park, so I just stopped somewhere out front. My very dirty, ten-year-old station wagon was now rubbing bumpers with a blue BMW and a white Stingray.

I got the distinct feeling that I had probably underdressed.

I rang the doorbell and thought of how catastrophic it would be if it quit working. Nobody would ever hear a knock on a door in a place this large.

A butler answered. What else? Did I really expect anything else? He was young and bland. I called him James for lack of anything else to call him, and he didn't find me the least bit amusing.

I was led into the dining room, where I was left for several minutes. The dining room was in a classic baroque style, looking more like a church from the old country. I expected the table to be about forty feet long, but in truth it was only about twenty. There were two places set in an exquisite bone china, trimmed in gold. All of this for lunch. I'd love to see what he did for dinner.

The contrast to what Norah Zumwalt had lived in was striking. I found it hard to imagine her ever living here. Her home, granted, was no dump, but it paled seriously in comparison.

"Sorry to keep you waiting."

I spun around to find, I assumed, Harold Zumwalt standing in the entryway. He was in a white suit with a strawberry red tie. He had a heavy but perfectly cut beard. He was average height and weight, but had extraordinary silver eyes surrounded by thick, short lashes.

"No problem," I said. I didn't mind waiting alone. It gave me a chance to gawk in private.

He never offered to shake my hand. He only waved for me to sit down, and like magic, our soup arrived. I have no idea what kind of soup it was, but it was delicious. I kept waiting for him to make some sort of effort at small talk, but he did not. He said nothing. We ate in silence. I couldn't stand it. I mean, he'd asked me here for a reason, hadn't he? Maybe I should ask him if he had a garbage disposal.

"I don't mean to be rude," I said, "but I can't believe that Norah ever lived here."

"She didn't. We had a much smaller home in Webster Groves. She never knew the extent of my wealth."

"Why did you keep it a secret?" I questioned.

"Because I didn't want her to marry me for the money. If money was the motive, I never could have trusted her. After we were married, I kept it from her because then I would be vulnerable to her. I would have a chink in my armor." He wiped his mouth with the linen napkin. "I gave her the house, with the agreement that she would not take me to court for any more, and that she would not touch my personal accounts. I paid her alimony, of course."

"Of course," I echoed sarcastically. I couldn't help but think that good old-fashioned greed was what drove him to keep his wealth a secret from her. "What a slap in the face that was to her, when she found out," I said.

"Until you've lived in our world, Mrs. O'Shea, don't be so quick to judge."

I looked down at my soup, dutifully chastised. Why was it that he and Jeff could make me feel so little? One thing was for sure: The old kill-your-wife-for-the-insurance motive seemed pretty ridiculous at the moment.

Our lunch arrived: veal, which I didn't touch. A pasta with a clam sauce and a steamed vegetable made up the rest of the entrée. I picked at my food, not really eating but a few bites. Zumwalt was upsetting me. The muscles around my stomach were getting tighter and tighter.

I watched Zumwalt as he ate, meticulously raising his fork to his mouth with the greatest concentration. He chewed each bite at least twenty times, and ate with proper etiquette, knife in the right hand, fork in the left and upside down.

This man was, without a doubt, the most anal-retentive human being I had ever met. He probably slept in ironed pajamas, with slippers next to the bed, not one millimeter out of sync with each other.

"So why did you call me here? Surely not to show me how wealthy and influential you are."

"On the contrary," he began.

Does anybody ever really say "on the contrary"?

Zumwalt looked to the ceiling for divine guidance. "I invited you over to ask you to—how do you say it in river language—lay off?"

River language? "Are you suggesting that I'm from a different social class, Mr. Zumwalt?"

"I just want to make sure that you can understand what I'm about to say. I want no misunderstandings."

I felt a tingle on the back of my neck. Was he about to threaten me? "What? What do you want me to understand?"

"Your private crusade, Mrs. O'Shea. End it. You and Sheriff Brooke are causing great waves on my peaceful ocean," he said.

"So get a surfboard. Look, I don't know what kind of game you're playing, but I would say that Sheriff Brooke must be getting close to something or you wouldn't have gone to all of this trouble just to tell me to lay off. What are you hiding?"

"Let us just say that if too much of an investigation was made on my family, we could be severely hurt. And we have a lot to lose."

I watched him closely as he swirled the wine in his glass as if it were Kool-Aid, and he had to mix the sugar up.

"Who killed her?" I asked.

"I don't know."

"Then what could be so bad that Sheriff Brooke's investigation could uncover?"

"You're the instigator here. Sheriff Brooke was taken care of until you came along and made him think differently." He laid his fork and knife across the ends of his plate, and then crossed his hands together. "Several years before our divorce, our family sought counseling."

Could I really be this lucky?

"I warn you, if any of this leaks out, I will know where it came from," he said. "I will ruin you," he said. He smiled at me, cold and calculating. "There were several reasons for the counseling. The main one was the children. Norah was having great difficulty with them in their early teenage years. Rita was jealous of everybody and everything, and Jeff was as obsessive as Rita was jealous."

Hold everything.

He couldn't possibly be talking about the same Rita and Jeff. They barely acted like they *had* personalities, much less enough of one to be neurotic. Maybe Zumwalt was trying to throw the suspicion off of himself.

Rain began to splatter against the window and he got up to look out. He spoke to the window, not me. "I also had a problem, one that I still indulge in. I like women, Mrs. O'Shea. . . ."

"That's great. Most men do." I was worried. I wasn't prepared to hear his confession. Besides, the bad guy usually confesses to all sorts of dastardly things, right before he kills or attempts to kill whomever it is he's confessing to.

"Yes. I agree," he said. "But I like mine in unusual ways. Let's say some people wouldn't understand my preferences."

"Are you a pervert?" I asked. "Is that what you're trying to say to me? What? You like to hurt women, is that it?" I was on my feet now, purse in hand and ready to run.

"You're afraid," I said. "You're afraid that if somebody finds out that you like to hurt women, they'll think that you killed Norah. Right? By giving her the ultimate pain. Am I right? They'd hang you up. No amount of evidence or lack of it could save you. The press would have a field day."

He swung around, eyes full of poison. "You don't know what that kind of information could do to me."

"I understand perfectly well what that kind of information could do to you. I can hear the gas pellets dropping now," I said. "Or maybe the sizzle of the electric chair."

"It could destroy my reputation," he sputtered. "I'd never work again!"

"Good! Good, I'm glad. How come perverts and psychopaths want to inflict pain and suffering, but never think they should have to pay the price? When the tables are turned, it's not very funny, is it?"

I was yelling now, and I could just imagine all the servants piled up on the other side of the door, peeping through the keyhole, trying to hear or see what was going on.

"I'm warning you," he said.

"Fine, warn me. I don't do very well with overbearing, perverted male authority figures. You know, kind of makes my skin crawl." I moved to the door. "So this is what money buys. The ability to be a pervert and get by with it. Well, you can keep your demented world, Mr. Zumwalt."

I was headed for the entryway when he called after me, "You are investigating the wrong family member. Tell Sheriff Brooke to halt or you will both be very sorry."

All the way out to my car, my only concern was that he had poisoned me. The next thing I knew, I was on Clayton Road headed for Interstate 270, glad to be back in the real world. It was as if I'd been trapped in the Twilight Zone.

Why? Why the confession? Maybe it was to let me know what and who I was dealing with. He had no reason to kill Norah, unless it was the result of an argument that got out of hand. But I found it hard to believe that an argument gone awry would end in several stab wounds. Usually, the victims just get hit over the head, pushed down the steps, or strangled. Believe me, I've been angry enough to want to strangle somebody before. But after stabbing somebody a few times, don't you think you'd stop yourself and go, "Is she dead yet?" Why go any higher?

He had risked a lot by confiding his secret to me. There was the chance that I would run and tell everything that I knew, and he took that chance to clear himself of the murder, no matter how much it implicated him in other things.

I am not a detective, I reminded myself. I wasn't trained to look for lies in every sentence. Could Zumwalt be using my naïveté to throw the suspicion elsewhere? Sheriff Brooke would not take this the same way that I had.

THE NEWS YOU MIGHT MISS
by Eleanore Murdoch

What's this? It is a sad, sad day for me when I have to report the kind of information that our native Colette Bourneville is reporting up in crime-infested St. Louis.

Torie and Rudy O'Shea had a break-in! Here. In New Kassel! First a murder in Wisteria, which is only ten miles away, and now a break-in! Sad, sad, sad. Torie's mother, Jalena Keith, said that the only thing they had been robbed of was their peace of mind.

Speaking of Jalena Keith, her blackberry cobbler won first place at the Bake-Off last Saturday at Pierre's. Are we surprised? I'm not.

Well, since school is out, I just want to tell everybody to be especially careful with their children until the floodwater goes down. If it ever goes down.

And Father Bingham was happy to report that people are sinning as much as ever. He had twenty-four people in his confessional last week, and a nearly full congregation for both masses on Sunday morning.

The Lord delivers, Father Bingham.

Until next time.

Eleanore

Sixteen

Sheriff Brooke sat crammed in a desk chair that looked as if it came from the local grade school. We sat in front of the microfilm reader in the New Kassel library. I had asked Aunt Bethany to keep the film indefinitely, thinking I might have to use it again.

"Here it is," I said. I found the article on the murdered woman. "Read it."

He acted stupid for a minute, as if he didn't know how to read, and then reached into his shirt pocket and pulled out his reading glasses. He looked embarrassed and then cleared his throat and began to read.

> "A neighborhood is in shock. The body of twenty-year-old Gwen Geise was found in a neighbor's barn Tuesday morning. The barn was on the property of Simon Jaffe. Miss Geise's throat had been cut from ear to ear. Sergeant William Heinze of the Partut County Police Department says there are no suspects as of yet. No motive has been revealed either."

Sheriff Brooke sat back and said nothing.

"Okay, in 1942, Eugene Counts lived in St. Mary's and Michael Ortlander lived in Pine Branch. I'm assuming they knew each other from church, because Eugene's father preached at the Pine Branch Church," I said.

"Where is Ortlander's mother?" he asked.

"In Progress, which is in Partut County."

"Vitzland is in Ste. Genevieve County?"

"Yes. I know what you're thinking. If you had switched identities with somebody, why would you come back to the same area?" I said.

"Exactly," he said as he took off his glasses. "It makes no sense. When did he come back to the States?"

"I don't know. Howie might be able to help on that one."

"Who is Howie?" he asked.

"Howard Braukman. He works for the National Personnel Records. He was how I found out that Ortlander was alive in the first place, even though I thought he was Eugene Counts at the time. But I think Ortlander would have come back in the last twenty years. Sometime in the 1970s."

"Why?"

"Maybe he thought that he had aged enough that nobody would recognize him as Michael Ortlander," I said.

"Yup. And he figured that everybody that knew Eugene Counts would either be dead or wouldn't care anymore."

I forwarded the microfilm machine to the same year but three days later. Sure enough, there was a notice of her burial.

> Friends and family buried Gwen Geise today. The twenty-year-old schoolteacher from Partut County was found dead in Maple Grove, in the west part of Partut County, on Tuesday. Investigators say they have a few leads and maybe even a suspect, although they won't elaborate. Internment was at the Yount Cemetery.

Sheriff Brooke sighed heavily. "I think I'll call the Partut County sheriff and see if I can have a look at the record for her murder. Who knows? Maybe Sergeant Heinze is still alive and I could talk to him."

"You think Ortlander killed Norah?"

"I think it's a pretty good possibility. I mean, we know that

Norah put the ad in the paper. I think she suspected that her father was alive even before she contacted you. Once you told me about the ad in the paper, that summed it up for me. Somehow, she suspected," he said. "He's the only one with any real motive to kill Norah. I have to admit," he said, rubbing his eyes and yawning, "I'm not so sure I would dismiss John Murphy as easily as you did."

"He just doesn't seem to have a big enough motive."

He rolled his eyes to the ceiling. "People have been killed for milk money," he said. "There is always the possibility that it was random. We can't forget that. There may not be a logical explanation for her murder. It's something you have to live with."

"No. I refuse to think that way. If it was random, I wouldn't have had that message left on my computer."

"Did you ever think that maybe it was Harold Zumwalt or Jeff—oh hell, Rita for that matter? Maybe they don't want you uncovering family skeletons. They don't care if you find her murderer, one way or the other. They just want you to stop snooping! Your break-in could have had nothing to do with Norah's actual murder!"

He raised his voice a little on that one. Aunt Bethany glanced over, and I waved to her.

"Let's get copies of these and I'll see what I can do about getting ahold of that police record," he said.

I was satisfied with that. It seemed for the first time since all of this began that we had a solid suspect. I hadn't told Sheriff Brooke about having lunch with Zumwalt, but what did it matter?

"One more thing," I said. "Did you investigate Cora Landing?"

He had a peculiar look on his face. I sensed that he really didn't want to answer me. "It was a dead end."

"Bull spit." Aunt Bethany frowned at me on that one. I hadn't actually said the word, but I suppose it sounded enough like it to get me into trouble.

Sheriff Brooke smiled nervously at her.

"There is no point in getting us thrown out of the library, for Christ's sake," he said.

"She's my aunt. She won't throw me out. She'll just tell my mother," I answered him. "There is more to Cora Landing than you're telling me."

"She's a beautician," he said.

"Do you expect me to believe that Norah had an appointment to get her hair done? If it was that easy, you would have just said that outright. Now, who is she?"

"She's John Murphy's lover."

"What?"

"Yes, but she wasn't with him on that night."

"Then what? John Murphy was cheating on his mistress? Having an affair with an affair? He said he was with a woman that night."

"That's what he told you. Until he's named her to us, he has no alibi."

"I don't understand," I said.

"It's possible he has no other alibi, and he just told you that to get you to shut up and leave his office."

"Then why was Norah meeting her?"

"I'm assuming that Norah confronted Cora over the affair."

"What about Cora? She could be a suspect."

He glanced around the library nervously. "I've considered it, but it's not the usual female method of killing somebody. Besides, she was in a diner with her entire bridge club the morning that Norah was killed."

I hate it when people burst my bubble.

•

I thought about Cora Landing the entire time I got groceries. I also thought about her the whole way home. I had this feeling that I'd end up speaking to Cora Landing before this was all over. Just to satisfy my own curiosity.

I turned left onto River Point Road and pulled into my drive. For a second I wondered why there were no lights on in the house. I reminded myself not to panic. After all, we had had the alarm installed a few days earlier. I remembered that my mother had gone into St. Louis County to visit a friend of hers, and Rudy, who'd come home from his business trip two days before, had taken the girls to his brother's house. I felt funny about this though, because it was around six-thirty in the evening and neither Rudy nor my mother had mentioned anything about staying for dinner.

I carried in the groceries, leaving out the chicken. When everybody came home, we could eat. To give Rudy more time, I took a shower.

It was after seven, and still nobody was home. I was getting angrier by the minute. I ended up eating a cupcake and drinking a flat Dr Pepper for dinner. Not that I would normally eat that sort of thing for dinner. I was feeling dejected and forgotten, so I had to eat something dreadful so that I could use it against them when they finally did come home. "Look, I had to eat a cupcake for dinner." Poor pitiful me. Rachel and Mary would probably congratulate me.

Okay, anger and self-pity soon gave way to genuine worry. I called Rick's house, and Rudy had left over three hours earlier. Rick lives in Meyersville, about twenty minutes away. Where was Rudy? Here is where I became a paranoid psycho of some sort.

In the span of ten minutes I envisioned him dead, and my children kidnapped. Or he could have had an accident and they were all dead. From there I went to imagining how I would tell his mother that her son had died, and to whom I would give his godforsaken ties. Then came the funeral. And there I was crying over three caskets that, of course, were a figment of my extraordinarily delusional mind!

Okay, I was calm. What if . . . what if he was with another woman? I had been acting weird lately. I hadn't been giving him or the girls the proper amount of attention. What if he was really at a lover's house, leaving *my* children in the car while they consummated their meeting? Or worse yet . . . he took my children inside. . . .

How do I do this to myself?

There was probably a perfectly logical explanation for why nobody had seen him or my two children in three hours. At the moment, though, the only explanations that I could come up with were hysterical ones.

Then I stopped. I had been so preoccupied with carrying out Rudy's castration sentence in my mind that I hadn't noticed how excruciatingly quiet it was. I stood in the middle of the kitchen with the hair raised on my arms. It was too quiet. Something wasn't right.

I walked out onto the back porch and breathed deeply, the fragrance of my roses soothing me. The sun was setting directly over my cherry tree, just beyond the chicken coop.

Now I noticed it.

Where were the chickens? They weren't out in the courtyard, clucking or pecking at the ground.

That was the whole point. I couldn't see or hear anything, except the crickets, and their song had become so loud in my ears that I thought I'd gladly go deaf.

"Here chickie chickies." I was calling for chickens. I was convinced that I had lost my blooming mind for sure. My voice cut through the silence in the backyard with a resounding echo.

Slowly, I walked down the sidewalk to the chicken coop. I lifted the latch on the courtyard door. I thought I heard a muffled cluck or two. I walked over to the building where their nests were, my heart thudding.

The door was shut and I had to yank, with my foot on the side of the building, to get it to open. Every chicken I owned came flying at me, squawking and pecking. I screamed from the sheer fright of having two dozen chickens fly in my face.

I jumped back and the gate to the courtyard rammed me in the back, and I screamed all over again because of that. The chickens were spastic, running around the courtyard. How long had they been locked up? It couldn't have been an accident. What were the chances of every single chicken being inside when the door shut?

Shut so hard that it was stuck, I reminded myself.

I overreact to everything, right?

My steps back to the house were quick but cautious. How long had I been in the house by myself? An hour? Two? Nothing had happened to me while I was in there. My God, I had even taken a shower.

I was just paranoid. Still, when I reached the steps that lead to the porch, I was trembling. The house no longer seemed to be mine. It no longer seemed to be the one that I had lived in since I was a child. It took on the eeriness of a dark abandoned piece of property. A stranger.

I slithered in the back door and stood in the kitchen, looking at everything. Was anything out of place? Was that coffee cup on the counter before? Of course it was. The area rug in the living room was turned up on one end. Did I do that? Was it like that when I got home?

My hand was on the banister, ready to head upstairs. The faces from the family portraits and baby pictures all looked down at me from the wall. This was my home. Those were my photographs. I felt brave for a second and ascended the steps without stopping. If I had stopped, I would not have gone all the way up.

Maybe my paranoia was a built-in defense mechanism, to warn me of the dangers. Now that was a paranoid statement if I ever heard one.

I looked at my desktop. The box from Rita was on the floor now, instead of being on the desk. Did I move that? Damn, damn, damn. Why couldn't I remember?

Maybe it's Harold, Jeff—oh hell, it could even be Rita for that matter. . . . Sheriff Brooke's words rang through my ears. *Maybe they don't want you uncovering their family skeletons.*

I reached for the phone and dialed 911, but never got to speak to the operator, who had come on the line. Something fell downstairs. I wasn't sure what it was—it sounded like a thud. Whoever had locked my chickens up was still there. In the house.

I was scared. I don't own a gun. Even my butcher knives are dull. I had no real way to protect myself. And a terrible thought

133

wormed its way into my mind. . . . What if the reason Rudy couldn't be found was because somebody had got to him?

I heard the noise again. As far as I could figure, I had three choices: I could wait upstairs and hope the police got there first. I could confront whatever it was downstairs and try to get out the door. Or I could jump out the window and hope that the paramedics would find me.

I wasn't brave enough for any of the above suggestions, so I opted to hide in the closet.

It was really quite an eye-opening experience being in the closet, trying to disappear into the floor. Ouch! What was I sitting on? It was Rudy's watch that had been missing for several weeks. My claustrophobia was about to get the best of me when I heard something coming from the office. It was unmistakably a person, walking toward the closet. Of course, if I were a killer, the first place I'd look would be under the bed or in the closet. I'd have to do better next time. If there was a next time.

My palms were sweaty and my mouth was dry. I thought I might pee in my pants as well. What is it about fear that makes your bodily fluids go crazy?

"Torie?"

Shit.

The closet door swung open, and there stood Rudy, Rachel, and Mary all looking down at me like I had horns growing out of my head.

"Look, honey," I said. "I found your watch."

Seventeen

I must admit, I felt pretty ridiculous when I realized that I had called the police for a coop of spastic chickens. You should have heard me trying to explain it to Deputy Newsome.

"Well, sir. See, I have this chicken coop and all of the chickens were inside of it."

His young face lit up as he said, "Why didn't you just let them out?"

It took a while, but he finally realized that I was getting at the fact that nobody here had done it. There must have been some strong vibes emanating from Rudy and me, because Deputy Newsome took down his information quickly and was out the door.

Rudy glared at me. I hate it when he glares at me. I always feel guilty, even when I haven't done anything wrong.

"I can't believe you," he said.

"What can't you believe?" I asked. I was the picture of innocence.

"For Pete's sake, Torie. You were hiding in the closet!"

"I know. I have terrible claustrophobia. Don't you feel the least bit sorry for me?"

"No! This is not like you to overreact like this."

"Overreact? Somebody locked the chickens in the coop," I said.

"You don't know that. How do you know that it wasn't a teenager playing a prank?"

"Because it wasn't," I said. "Rudy, don't you feel any sympathy for what I went through today? You know, it's not every day that a watch tries to give me an enema! It was very traumatic, I assure you. And just where the hell were *you?*"

"Oh, now you're going to try and switch the blame to me?" he asked. His cheeks were slowly turning red with every sentence.

"Well? If you'd been here—besides, nobody has seen hide nor hair of you in almost four hours!"

"I was buying you an anniversary present," he stated.

"Oh."

"And why don't you tell me why I spent all that money on an alarm system and it wasn't even activated?" he asked.

"What did you get me? Flowers?"

"Did you show your mother how to turn on the alarm? What am I thinking?" he said aloud. "Jalena can't even retrieve the messages off of the answering machine."

"Jewelry?"

"I bought you tickets to the symphony," he said, defeated.

I gasped. "What? You hate the symphony. What are we going to hear? Mozart? Chopin?"

A crooked smile played at the corners of his mouth. "Rachmaninoff," he said.

"The Rhapsody?" I said, stunned.

"Yup. Did I do good?" he asked.

"Oh my god, I don't believe it! Honey, you're the best," I said, and then kissed him.

"I know," he said. He looked genuinely pleased with himself and terribly smug. "Now, don't you feel the least bit of sympathy for *me?* I come home with a great surprise for you and you're hiding in the bedroom closet, claiming some deranged psychopath has locked up all your chickens."

He has such a way of putting things that makes me feel so ridiculous.

I did what he wanted me to do. I apologized for my behavior and told him he was right. But in my mind I knew better. Somebody had locked my chickens in the coop. And I thought it was one of the members of the Zumwalt family.

I decided that I would go see Jeff Zumwalt. It was very late in the evening, but I didn't care. It was stupid of me to go there, because there was the chance that Rudy was right and nobody had done anything to my chickens on purpose. But I couldn't forget that my other break-in had been very real. I needed to let the Zumwalts know that they could not intimidate me—although I was beginning to feel slightly intimidated.

Jeff looked shocked when he answered the door. Every time I saw him, his perfect good looks always caught me off guard.

"Mrs. O'Shea?" he asked.

"Yes."

"To what do I owe this visit?"

He didn't invite me in, which was just as well.

"Sheriff Brooke seems to think that a member of your illustrious family is trying to frighten me because I've uncovered a few things in your family that are less than ideal."

"You don't say?"

"Well, if you're innocent of this, I apologize, of course. And I'm not threatening you in any way. I just want you to know that anything your father has told me will not ever get out. It will not make it to the papers or the evening news."

"My father?"

"Yeah, he invited me—"

"Stay away from my father," he snapped. A slight but dangerously maniacal look played across his face, and then it was gone. "You have no business messing in my family. I've been more than patient with you. I had no idea that a stupid family tree was supposed to be so thorough."

"Fine."

As I turned to leave, he said one more thing. "It's interesting the way you completely overlook the obvious."

I started to explain to him how my mother had taught me that the obvious isn't always the answer, but I knew I'd be wasting my breath, so I asked what he wanted me to ask. "And what am I overlooking?"

"John Murphy."

"I'm not going to get into all of this here and now. I'm calling a truce, Jeff. Leave me and my family alone, and I'll leave yours alone."

Turning my back on him was one of the hardest things I've ever done because I thought he could kill me with the stare that he gave me. But I felt better. If Jeff had been trying to scare me because of finding the carefully hidden skeletons in their closets, I felt he would quit now. He had nothing to gain by keeping it up.

•

The next morning my mother tore into me for going to Jeff Zumwalt's house. I hadn't been scolded this good since I hid Nana's false teeth when I was in the eighth grade. Of course, it was the fact that I had hid them in the kitty-litter box that really got me into trouble. There could have been a few other times since then that she tore into me fairly good, but certainly not with such urgency as she did now.

"Don't you watch the news? Crazies are burying people in their backyards, and the people are never heard from again. Don't you ever listen to the speeches that you give your children? You should not have gone alone, especially."

The telephone rang, and I was delighted to answer it.

"Torie, it's me, Colin."

"Yes." I prepared myself to listen to his speeches as well, until I realized that he didn't know that I had gone to Jeff's house the night before.

"Any more incidents since last night?"

"No." Sheriff Brooke was one of the few people who believed that two dozen chickens all being in the chicken coop at the same time was too much of a coincidence.

"Well, I got the file on the Gwen Geise case."

"And?"

"Meet me at Velasco's in about two hours," he said, and hung up the phone.

I wanted to see Rita today. I hadn't had a chance to talk to her since I had lunch with her father, and I felt I should speak to her before Jeff did.

And no, nothing my mother said did any good. I will have to remember this when my children get older.

I changed into my blue sundress and brown sandals and decided that I'd go by and see Rita after I'd met with Sheriff Brooke. But I had one stop to make before going to see either one of them.

•

It was a long shot. But Sheriff Brooke had told me that Cora Landing was a beautician. I spent an hour on the phone, calling every beauty shop in the phone book for St. Louis and St. Louis County, asking to have an appointment made with Cora. I finally hit the jackpot, at a place called Heads R Us.

When I entered the salon in south county, an older woman smiled at me over a pair of scissors and let me know that she'd be right with me. The salon was decorated in pink and green, and giant plastic scissors separated each workstation. It also stunk from the perm solution, and my eyes began to water.

I told the woman I wanted to see Cora and she went to get her for me.

There were only three girls working, and judging by their ages, I picked out the one that I thought was Cora. I was dead wrong. I expected it to be the fortyish woman, with stylish hair and fingernails the color of watermelon.

Instead, Cora Landing was younger than I was, and a hell of a lot better looking, too. I was tempted to ask her if she was a *Playboy* model. When John Murphy cheated, at least he did it with style. She walked up to the counter, looking at my hair. I assumed she was deciding what kind of cut she'd like to give me.

"Did you have an appointment?" she asked me.

"No. Are you Cora?"

"Yes."

"I was wondering if there was someplace that we could talk?" I asked, watching her look at me with surprise.

"Why?" she asked. Sparkling green eyes watched me cautiously. She had tons of blond hair, most likely the result of one of those painful little caps that you pull your hair through. Shiny red lipstick was applied generously, and she was about a foot taller than I.

"I'm a friend of John Murphy."

"Oh, Jesus, are you a cop?"

"No. I was also a friend of Norah's. If you refuse to speak to me, fine. I'll understand. But I really only need about two minutes of your time."

She hesitated before answering. Glancing over her shoulder she said, "As long as I can smoke."

"Sure."

"Cheryl! I'm goin' for a smoke," she yelled at her boss.

We stepped outside, and the dismal gray clouds separated long enough to give us a few minutes of much needed sunshine. "Okay, make it quick," she announced.

"Were you with John Murphy the morning that Norah was killed?"

"I already told the cops that I wasn't," she said as she puffed on her cigarette.

"Who was?"

"How should I know?"

"Why did you meet with Norah the night before she was killed?"

"She called me. Said she knew about John and me, and she wanted to talk. First I thought, I don't need this shit. But then she said she'd come to work and camp on the doorstep if I didn't see her. So I figured, what the hell?" she said. She finished one cigarette and started another.

"And?"

"When she got to my house, all she asked me about was the other other woman that he was seeing. I said, 'Well, shit, lady.' I didn't know that he was doin' anybody else but me and her."

"What did she say to that?"

"Nothing really. She just kept asking me if I knew what kind of car that she drove. What she looked like. Had I ever seen her before. Maybe at John's office? Those kinds of things."

Why would Norah be so obsessed about another "other woman" if she wasn't obsessed with Cora? If she was worried about being able to compete with them, Cora would be the one to be jealous of.

"Did she seem upset about you and John?"

"She didn't ask me or beg me to stay away from him, if that's what you're drivin' at. I tell you, this is not what I bargained for."

"What do you mean?"

"This guy tipped me off one night about John. Said he knew him and that the guy was hurting real bad. You know, he could use a lady friend."

"Where were you when this happened?" I asked.

"At a bar. Don't ask me which one 'cause I done forgot. Anyway, so I figure, he's a nice-looking guy. So I go over, start talking to him. We hit it off. I mean, I really liked him," she said, inhaling. "Next thing I know, I get a call from Norah asking me to meet with her. She's dead the next day," she said. She let out the smoke that she had been holding. It curled around her head, resembling a sort of laurel wreath. "I mean, freaky shit," she said, shivering.

The woman definitely had a way with words.

"How long had you been seeing John when Norah contacted you?" I asked. I had no specific game plan to my inquiry. I just thought if I could keep Cora talking, eventually she'd hit on something that I needed.

"A few weeks."

"I'm just a bit confused. How do you suppose that Norah knew about you?"

"Woman knows when her man's cheatin'."

"Well, yes. Normally, I'd agree with you. But rarely does a woman know her name and phone number and place of business. How did Norah find you? How did she know who you were?"

I could tell that the thought had never entered her mind before now. She seemed genuinely puzzled by the whole thing.

"Maybe she found my name and number in John's things and just assumed the rest," she said.

It was possible. But Norah had not lived with John nor worked with him. I couldn't help but wonder just how much access she would have had to his personal things, and wonder also at the large coincidence in finding Cora's name and number. John didn't seem like the type to be that messy or careless.

"What was the last thing that Norah said to you?"

"Thank you for your time."

"Do you think she knew who the other woman was?" I asked.

"Yes. Why else would she be so interested in her?" She threw her cigarette butt on the ground and smashed it with her navy blue heels.

"And you have no idea who the mystery lady was?" I asked.

"The only thing I can think of was one evening when I was at John's office, a woman drove up in a red car all mad about something."

"Was it Norah?" She nodded negative. "How do you know that the woman was angry?" I asked.

"She damned near ran over us. Came out of nowhere like she was waiting in the parking lot the whole time."

"Did you get a good look at her? Could you describe her to me?" I asked persistently.

"No. She called John a bunch of names and took off. He ran after her, she stopped, they screamed at each other, she took off again."

"Did he explain who she was to you?"

"Didn't ask, he didn't explain." She looked around nervously. "Look, my cig is smoked. I need to go back to work."

"Sure thing," I said. "And thank you very much. It means a lot to me."

"Yeah, whatever," she said. She headed back toward the building.

"By the way," I said. "Do you really play bridge?" I asked her.

I found it very difficult to imagine Miss July sitting around playing bridge on Fridays.

"Love it."

•

Sheriff Brooke sat in a booth in the corner of Velasco's. He was off duty. At least, I assumed that he was because he wasn't in uniform and he was drinking a beer. It was one of those dark beers that look more like beef broth than a brew.

I sat down across from him, and he pushed the file toward me. That action alone sparked my imagination. I felt as if I were in a spy movie, and couldn't help but glance around the dining room looking for a man in a trench coat and sunglasses and holding a newspaper.

"You can either stomach through the grotesque details and photographs, or let me summarize them for you."

Staring at the yellowed folder, I flashed back to the day I found Norah Zumwalt. Since finding her, I've had a terrible aversion to red.

"You do the honors," I said, pushing the folder back at him.

Just then, Kurt Emery came to our table. Kurt is African American, and attending Washington University Medical School. He's about twenty-four and works at Velasco's half of his life so that he can go to Washington University the other half. He was dressed in jeans and a shirt that said, "Just Too Sexy."

Velasco's is a jeans and T-shirt type of place.

He pulled up a chair from an empty table and straddled it. "What can I get for you today, Torie?"

"Kurt, you know the sheriff?" I asked.

"Of course," he said. He nodded at Sheriff Brooke, who nodded back.

"I hear that Sylvia is having heart failure over the museum," Kurt said to me.

"Why?" I asked. I suddenly realized that I hadn't talked to Sylvia or Wilma in quite a few days.

143

"Something about she wanted to do a display of original documents that concerned the different founding families of New Kassel, for the museum opening."

"So? What's the problem?"

"She's lost a whole file or something," he said as he rested his chin on the back of the chair.

"Oh, she probably just doesn't remember where she put it. I'll go over in the morning and help her find it," I said.

Kurt laughed. It was a sneaky sort of laugh, the kind that teenage boys give in the classroom when the teacher has chalk dust on her nose or something. "She's pretty peeved at you," he said. "If you go over there, you better go with a broadsword and shield."

"I'll be careful. I've fought off Sylvia more than once," I said. Looking at Sheriff Brooke, I noticed he seemed a little agitated and had a death grip on the file. "Uh, Kurt. We'll have the special. Make it a large, extra cheese."

"Okay, whatcha want to drink?"

"The usual."

"Be right back," he said. He stood up and returned the chair to the other table.

"All right, do not repeat this," Brooke said. "Any of it." He glanced around the room, eyes landing on the jukebox. Velasco's can be very diversionary, as it is decorated with James Dean and Elvis Presley. The entire theme is 1950s. Chuck even went so far as to hang some of his old 45 records on the walls.

Sheriff Brooke gulped down half of his beer as I waited for him to begin.

"Gwen Geise was number three."

"What?"

"She was the third girl that year to be killed in the exact same manner. Except that she was the only one in Partut County. One took place just across the river, in southern Illinois, and the other in eastern Tennessee, which is just across the river as well."

"So they were all within what? An hour from Ortlander's home?"

"Yup," he said. "They were also raped."

"Oh, God."

"The authorities were very successful about keeping the details out of the papers. For one reason, the Tennessee woman was the governor's daughter. He paid big money to keep the rape part quiet," he said. "Sergeant Heinze nearly lost it on this one."

"I suppose every cop must have a case that haunts him," I said. "What's yours?"

"This one, if I don't nail the bastard," he said. He drank the last of his beer. Running his fingers through his hair, he sat back against the booth. "I talked to the captain down there who was a rookie when Sergeant Heinze retired. He said that Heinze is dead now, so I can't even talk to him."

"Was Ortlander one of the suspects?" I asked.

"He was at the top of the list. Ortlander knew the girl well and was seen with her the day she disappeared. Heinze didn't have enough evidence to arrest him. Ortlander took off for the war and never came back."

"So Heinze thought that his suspect got killed and dropped the investigation."

"Yup. I have to admit, I never would have made the connection to Eugene Counts if it weren't for you. And I never would have known that he was actually Ortlander. I'm indebted to you."

"Don't mention it." I suddenly felt incredibly guilty that I'd been keeping things from him. "So you think that Ortlander killed Norah? She wasn't raped, nor were the wounds alike."

"Well, if he did kill these women, which we can safely assume considering Eugene Counts was killed with the same type of wound, I think it establishes that he is capable of committing Norah's murder."

"Heartbreak Hotel" came blaring from the jukebox. "Have there been any other murders with this modus operandi in the last ten years?"

"No. But if he's still killing, he may have changed his MO or just made sure the bodies were never found."

Chills went down my spine. This was giving me the heebie-jeebies. "Why get sloppy now?"

"Sloppy? We have virtually nothing in the way of physical evidence. Granted, if I can get the okay to have him arrested, I might be able to match some fibers or something up to him. But I wouldn't say he was sloppy."

"Well, why not get rid of her body? Why not abduct her, kill her somewhere else, and dump the body? It doesn't seem like his style."

"Maybe he was frantic. Maybe she made the connection that he wasn't Eugene and confronted him, and he wanted her silenced immediately. Maybe he got interrupted and couldn't get rid of the body. There are all sorts of possibilities."

Kurt brought us our pizza. Mushroom, pepperoni, sausage, and onions. That was the Velasco Special, and it was the best pizza in a hundred miles.

"It's hot," Kurt said.

We ate in silence for a few minutes. Sheriff Brooke seemed to enjoy the pizza thoroughly.

"Okay, all right. I confess," I said.

"What to?" he asked. "Damn, this pizza's good."

"I had lunch with Zumwalt. Don't look at me like that. He invited me."

"Did he confess to the murder of his ex-wife?"

"Don't give me that condescending attitude, Sheriff. Of course he didn't confess."

"Well, John Murphy confessed to you but not to us, that he was having an affair. I just thought maybe Zumwalt might follow his example."

"Murphy told me he was having an affair so that I could lay my own demons to rest. He had no intentions of any of you finding out. He told me he'd deny it if it got to police level."

"So? What did Zumwalt say?"

"He said we were investigating the wrong family member."

"Who does he want investigated? Jeff and Rita?"

"I can only assume," I said through a piece of pizza. "He alluded to a lot. And he told me everything with the risk of being exposed wholeheartedly as a pervert."

"They don't put you to death for being a pervert," he said.

"They should."

"Well, they don't. But they do put you to death for cold-blooded murder. I think I would choose the same way he did."

He always finds the string to unravel my carefully crafted theory.

"I'd like to talk to some of her employees at the antique shop," I said.

"We already did that."

"Yeah, but did you ask them about Jeff and Rita?"

"What do you know?" he asked.

"Nothing. Something just doesn't feel right, that's all."

Kurt came back to the table then, smiling his contagious smile. "Need anything else?"

"You can refill this soda for me. Otherwise we're okay," I said.

"Sure. Just leave when you're finished. You know your money isn't any good here."

Sheriff Brooke raised an eyebrow at that statement. I smiled sweetly. See? Some people like me.

"You tell that gorgeous mama of yours that I said hello," Kurt said as he walked away.

"I will."

Sheriff Brooke gave me a strange look. It was as if he had seen me for the first time.

"What?"

"Is there nobody in this town that looks at you the least bit objectively?"

"What the heck do you mean by that?"

"I think they should make you honorary mayor. You have the entire town eating out of your hand."

"I do not."

Do I?

After several moments of silent contemplation he finally said, "So, how is that gorgeous mother of yours?"

"Too old for you." Oh God, I couldn't believe I actually said that. I turned a deep red; I could tell by how hot my face suddenly became.

"You're so protective of her."

"Look, can we get back to the investigation here?"

"Hey, don't get any bright ideas. The only reason I shared this part about the girls with you was to show you how dangerous Ortlander is. I want you to promise you'll stay away from him."

"I have no intentions of ever going back to see him," I said.

"Good," he said. " 'Cause this is my investigation. You are a civilian and I could throw you in jail for interference."

"You won't," I said, and smiled. He did not smile at me. Instead he gave me the scowl that is his trademark.

I get the funny feeling that he hates me.

THE NEWS YOU MIGHT MISS
by Eleanore Murdoch

My deepest sympathies to Mayor Bill Castlereagh, whose restaurant, the Old Mill Stream, finally succumbed to Mother Nature. It is such a calamity. But thanks to our own Torie O'Shea, Elaine Dinwiddie, Chuck Velasco, and others, the Castlereaghs were able to save most of the contents within the building. The museum is opening soon. Volunteers are needed. Sign up at the Gaheimer House.

Ricky Reaves, owner of the Birk/Zeis Home, is pleased to announce that his wife gave birth to a darling little girl that looks just like him. He is particularly pleased that she looks nothing like his mother-in-law. After sixteen hours of labor, the beautiful girl weighed in at seven pounds and 14 ounces. They named her Katherine Rose. Until next time.

Eleanore

Eighteen

It was Friday morning and I was at my office at the historical society. It was too early for the Pershings, I was hoping. I thought I'd find Sylvia's missing file and catch up on some work before they came in, and maybe that would make up for my slacking off lately. Besides, my father and his buddies were coming for the jam session that night, and I wouldn't get anything done all weekend.

The Midwest had made the covers of every major news magazine that there was, because of the flood. Our levee was still holding, and it actually seemed like the water had gone down a few inches.

I thought I would do a flood theme for the museum opening. Surely there had been a flood in the past that made the news, and that would tie in quite interestingly. Sylvia kept all of the newspapers on file downstairs in the basement, so I headed down there to see what I could find.

It's not a basement, really. It's more of a cellar. The steps are just unfinished boards, and the floor and walls are concrete, resulting in a musty odor. A lightbulb hangs from the ceiling, exposing wires. I have no idea how Sylvia can stand to come down here.

Filing cabinet number one: nothing of interest. Filing cabinet number two: newspapers. I opened the drawer and inside was every page of every copy of the *New Kassel Gazette* that had ever been printed. Each one had been laminated so that it wouldn't tear or yellow, and was filed according to year.

Well, I didn't know what year a flood had occurred, so I would be there all day or I'd have to ask Wilma when she came in. But I was hoping to be finished before they came in. I glanced around the room, and my eyes landed on the filing cabinet on the other side of the room, which I had never looked in. It was the one filing cabinet that had no tags to tell me what was inside, and the one cabinet that was usually locked. Only this time, the top drawer was open by about an inch.

I opened the drawer and inside were files, with no headers, but neat, as all of Sylvia's records are.

Every file seemed to pertain to Hermann Gaheimer or the Gaheimer family in some way. One file even contained old photographs, one of which I recognized as being of Hermann Gaheimer.

Then I found it.

I, Hermann Gaheimer, being of sound body and mind, do hereby declare this, my last will and testament.

Cool. This would make a great display under glass at the museum. My eyes flicked down the page, and my heart caught in my throat.

I do hereby bequeath all of my worldly possessions, and the sum of one million, six hundred forty dollars, to my beloved Sylvia Pershing.

Holy cow. I dropped the piece of paper back into the file and slammed the drawer shut so fast, I barely got my hand out of the damn drawer. Sylvia Pershing! He left everything to Sylvia. Why the hell would he do that? What was it I was saying a while back about Sylvia couldn't possibly have known him that well?

Jesus, what had I found?

Just then I heard the door shut upstairs and couldn't believe my misfortune that one of the Pershing sisters, if not both, had come to work this early.

"Victory!" Sylvia shrilled. "Victory, are you here? If you don't answer, I'm going to get my gun and shoot whoever is driving your car, pretending to be you."

"Yes, Sylvia. I'm down here."

She descended the steps with more agility than I could muster. Her silver gaze scraped me from head to toe. "Whatever are you doing down here?"

Could she tell that I knew something that I wasn't supposed to know? Because it seemed like she knew what I was thinking.

"Uh, the flood. I thought I'd do a display under glass of the flood, and I wanted to tie in a flood from before, only I didn't know what year there was a flood before, or even if there was one. A flood, I mean. Was there one? I wonder. I mean you would know, wouldn't you? Being so old and everything. Not that I think you're terribly old. Just partially old."

"Victory, are you all right?" she asked me.

"Of course, never been better. Why do you ask?"

"Because you're acting like you're on some of those street drugs that I saw on *20/20* the other night."

"Huh, fancy that."

Her perusal of me became more intense. If I didn't get out of the basement soon, I would die.

"Victory, are you pregnant?"

"God, no," I said, giggling. "I mean, not that I couldn't be, because I could be. But rather that I'm not, because I know I'm not. At least, the last time I checked I wasn't."

"Nineteen forty-two," she said. "That was the last big flood. The mill and the Birk/Zeis Home had four feet of water in them. And the Murdoch Inn, which was a private residence I believe in 1942, had about the same. We didn't have a levee back then," she said, and headed back up the steps.

She stopped, looking at the filing cabinet on the other side of the room for what seemed like an eternity. It was as if she suddenly remembered that she had left it open or unlocked. And now it was shut. I finally got the guts to look her in the eye. She did not say a word, but rather communicated in silence.

The problem was, I was not certain what those silver eyes were trying to say to me.

Nineteen

It is impossible to sleep when a jam session is going on on the first floor of your home. At least, if you're over thirty. My children didn't seem to be the least bit deterred from their sleep and were actually snoring. Rudy had found that if he took his pillow and blanket out to the back porch he could get a few winks.

My father and his musical companions had pounded out six different versions of "Waltz across Texas." I was getting no sleep at all and couldn't see any in the near future. So if you can't beat 'em, join 'em. Which is what I always did as a child anyway. I pulled on my sweats and headed downstairs.

What the heck, I'd even have a beer.

Dad was situated on a kitchen chair that he had pulled into the living room, playing the guitar. I remember when I was a child, when Dad would sit on the couch and play, I would lie on his lap, between him and the guitar and feel the vibrations of the instrument. Eventually I would go to sleep. It is one of my most cherished memories.

Dad had his faults, but he had a good side, too. His bad side was that he liked to chase women, even when he was married. When he wasn't chasing women, he would disappear without a word, only to return in a week. He had usually been at a jam session. If he was home, he was having a jam session. Am I repeating myself here?

He's also a slob. I washed his coffee cup one time, quite by accident, and I had a crazed lunatic on my hands. I actually thought he was going to cry, because now it would take six months to get that much grime back in his mug. In the meantime, his coffee just wouldn't taste the same.

The good side of Dad was that he was a damn good musician. Could have been professional, but why he didn't would take up more time than I have to explain it. Let it suffice to say that it was his own doing.

He always provided for us. He has a wicked sense of humor and always taught me to be true to myself because I was who I had to face every morning in the mirror.

His brother, Uncle Melvin, played lead guitar. Uncle Melvin was the heartthrob of the family. In his younger days he had sandy brown hair that lay in perfect waves and ocean green eyes. No matter how much he ages, he will always have those gorgeous eyes.

Bob Gussey was nearly four hundred pounds and played the drums. I can never figure out how that little drummer's stool actually holds him. Pete Ramey played the bass. He was your suit-and-tie kind of guy with a needle nose that my grandmother could quilt with. Josh Rizzoni was on violin and occasional piano. He had—are you ready?—twelve children. He wasn't sure if they were all his, but he loved them all just the same.

All they were missing was a slightly woozy female with a halfway decent alto voice. Tonight, I filled the position for them.

I have no idea how many Patsy Cline songs I managed to butcher. I stopped counting at four. But I know I did a respectable version of Dinah Washington's "What a Difference a Day Makes."

Rudy stumbled in sometime around 3 A.M., long enough to be dutifully ashamed and embarrassed for me. I'd let him carry the brunt of shame because I was having entirely too much fun. I'd even brought my own lampshade. I was having so much fun, I wasn't thinking about Norah or Sylvia, none of it. I also wasn't keeping track of how many beers that I was drinking, which is dangerous because two will make me forget my name.

It was in this diversionary frolic that I lost myself completely. Until I heard it.

I was leaned over the arm of the couch watching the hair on Uncle Melvin grow, and listening to my dad moan out the words to a George Jones song. Something about a woman and a Corvette. Something like a man was complimenting another man on his car, and he really meant the woman in the front seat. A woman. A Corvette. Red Corvette. Red. Red. Red. Rita Schmidt.

I don't know why I hadn't made the connection before. It took the words of that song to bring it together in my properly pickled brain. Rita drove a red sports car. Cora had said that a woman in a red car had almost run them over in the parking lot.

I sat up on the couch as straight as I could without pitching myself forward. Rita was having an affair with her mother's boyfriend. I'd bet on it. That would certainly explain Norah's obvious obsession with confirming the identity of the other woman. I had a definite feeling that she knew who it was. She knew it was her daughter. It all made sense.

Oh God, how awful for Norah.

Oh God, my poor head.

•

If a human being has ever had a hangover, it must be pure stupidity that makes her repeat the act. Or else she figures, Oh, it won't happen to me.

Well, it happened.

It took me a half an hour that morning just to figure out why I was on my couch. Another half an hour went by before I realized how come there were so many ugly old men in the living room with me.

But it was nearly two o'clock in the afternoon before I remembered what it was that the George Jones song had triggered in my head the night before. Now things were starting to look very peculiar. I could not ignore the possibility that Michael Ortlander had murdered Norah. But if I was right about Rita and John, it certainly threw a new twist on things. Suddenly, the absence of an alibi really seemed condemning where John Murphy was concerned. Could Norah have confronted him about his affair with Rita and a fight evolved? Could John have gone nuts as a result of this argument and killed her? Could Rita have gone a little crazy when her mother found out? No, Rita had an alibi, I reminded myself.

I managed to eat a little something. Three pieces of plain bread and a glass of milk. Everybody has his magic cure-all for a hangover. Mine is bread and milk. I've only had to use it three or four times in my life. I must have been sitting at the kitchen table for half of the day. Mom came into the kitchen and opened the blinds, and even though the sky was gray and overcast, my pupils dilated, sending an incredible pain through my head.

"Aargh," I said.

"I can't believe you got drunk," Mom said in her best parental voice.

"I only had four beers. I don't remember intentionally setting out to get drunk," I said. "It just sort of happened. I got all caught up in the music."

"Now you know why I divorced your father."

Just then the guys in the living room picked up their instruments and started playing music all over again. How could they keep finding songs they hadn't already played? It was Saturday; this would go on until Sunday night, at least.

"That was the other reason," Mom added with a nod of her head toward the living room.

"Thank God Rudy doesn't play an instrument. I'm going to have him take the girls to his parents' house for the rest of the day. They have to be tired of hearing that," I said. "And the next time Dad calls and wants to borrow my house, make up an excuse. Tell him . . . the chickens are allergic to it or something."

"Won't have to. Bill called this morning and wasn't happy."

"Oh, it never occurred to me that he could hear the music that well. I mean, he is a couple of acres away."

"Well, he did. Also, Rita called. She said that she would be home today if you wanted to come by."

I said nothing for the longest time. I was too busy trying to figure out what it was that I was going to say to her. I'd been trying to get an appointment with her for a few days because I had wanted to talk with her since I'd seen her father. But now I suspected she was the one that John Murphy had been having the affair with. How could I bring up the subject without actually accusing her? And if I was wrong?

"You do want to see her, don't you?" Mom asked.

"You better believe it," I said. "I just don't know what to say to her," I said, swallowing hard at the bile rising in my throat.

"Instead of trying all of these concoctions not to throw up," she said, "why don't you just stick your finger down your throat and get it over with. Get the poison out of your system. You'll feel better. Just confront it," she said.

Why are mothers always trying to get the poison out of your system? If all the things in the world that supposedly caused poison in your system did actually exist, the human race would have died centuries ago.

"Works that way with people, too," she said. "Sometimes it's better if you just get the poison out, up front."

I hate it when my mother gets philosophical.

"Also, Wilma called."

"Wilma?" I asked apprehensively.

"She said to tell you that one of Norah's employees is Fern Kennard. She lives in those apartments off of Hanover and the outer road."

"Oh," I said. I had forgotten that I had asked Wilma and Sylvia if they knew any of Norah's employees. "Great."

"Is something wrong?" my mother asked.

"No."

I started to say something and decided not to. When I had managed to change my clothes and brush my teeth, I made my way though the amplifiers, instruments, and musicians to the front door. Taking a deep breath, I made it to my car.

Starting the car, I found a radio station that played some

good solid rock and roll. As much fun as I'd had, I'd listened to entirely too much crying-in-your-beer music. It's just too bad that I didn't do more crying in my beer than drinking it.

George Thorogood and the Destroyers pounded out the harsh chords to "Bad to the Bone." I sighed with relief.

I pulled into the parking lot of the Royal Court Apartments minutes later. The complex was clean and neat, with two stories. The tenants of Royal Court had access to a swimming pool and game room, and dinky apartments with one or two bedrooms, for four hundred bucks a month.

I had no idea which one Fern lived in, so I checked the names on the boxes in each building and I finally found an F. Kennard, number 23B. I headed to her apartment and hoped that I didn't look as rough as I felt. I hadn't put on any makeup, but at least I'd brushed my hair. I was wearing a pair of navy blue shorts and a plain, dark green shirt with white tennis shoes. No socks. I usually wear socks, but I didn't want to mess with them.

I rang the bell. Fern answered in seconds. When I saw her, I knew I had seen her around town. She was about sixty, with gray hair and eyeglasses from the 1960s. They weren't very thick, and pointed up on the ends.

"Ms. Kennard," I said in my most professional tone. "I was wondering if I could speak to you about Norah Zumwalt."

"Are you a cop?"

"No."

"A private dick?"

"A what?" I asked. Then, realizing that a private dick wasn't a venereal disease, but a private investigator, I answered, "No, just a friend. I'm Victory O'Shea." I extended a hand, which she took and shook graciously.

She opened the door all the way then and let me inside. Her apartment was small. The kitchen and living room ran together with just a breakfast bar to separate them. Over the sofa hung a very large painting of a poodle. I couldn't help but wonder if it was a monument to a former pet.

"I've already told the police everything I know," she said. Her dentures clicked as she spoke.

159

"How well did you know her?" I asked.

"I've worked for her since she owned the shop, about three years. If you're here to tell me that she was a drug lord or something, I don't want to hear it. I like to keep some illusions in my old age."

I couldn't help but chuckle. "No, nothing like that. I just want to know if she had any trouble at work. Bill collectors, any enemies? An irate ex-employee?"

"No. Her ex-husband paid her enough money that she didn't need to work. She was fairly well off so there were no troubles in the way of creditors. I just can't believe she was murdered," she said. "It's always a shock when somebody dies or is murdered, but I keep expecting her to call me. I want her to tell me in her soft voice that it was all a mistake," she said, and sniffled.

Believe me, I thought, it was no mistake.

"Did she have any fights with anybody the week she was murdered?"

"Well, I know she was always fighting with her kids. But, honey, who doesn't? She loved them, unconditionally. I don't think that they loved her like that, though. Her kids only loved her when she did what they wanted. Other than John, she didn't really have anybody else," she said.

"And there were no arguments bad enough to kill her over?" I asked.

"Lord no, nothing worth killing somebody over. But what do I know? Kids are killing each other over their jackets. Ridiculous, spoiled-rotten people, that's all I got to say."

I couldn't agree with her more.

"People don't know the value of life," she said.

"Have you heard of a woman named Cora Landing? Did you ever hear Norah mention her?"

"No."

"Did you know John Murphy very well?"

She grinned slightly. "I worked for her for a year and a half and didn't know she had a boyfriend. Come to find out, she'd been dating him for about seven years!"

"She acted okay with the relationship?" I asked.

"If there was anything wrong, she didn't let on. But then, I don't think she would have let it show even if there was something wrong. She was that type of person."

Yes, I was beginning to see. It seemed as though Norah had to keep up a happy facade. The portrait being painted of her life by friends and family was of a woman that couldn't be the fault of anything.

"Are you the woman that works at the Gaheimer House?" Fern asked me.

"Yes," I said. It is not unusual for people to know me and for me not to know them. This is a town whose very survival centers around its historical landmarks, its festivals. When you are involved in all of that, you get to be known even if it is only by name.

"Norah admired you so much," she said. "I thought your name was familiar."

"What do you mean Norah admired me? I'd barely ever spoken to her until about a week before she died, when she came to the office."

"Well, nonetheless. She knew who you were, and she used to say that if she could live anybody's life it would be yours."

I was dumbfounded. "Mine?" I barely got out.

"You have a great job," Fern said. "You have two wonderful children, you have a nice normal husband who supports you in your endeavors. She used to list the qualities," Fern said. "But the last one, and the one that meant the most to her, was that you know who you are. Norah never knew who she was," she said. "She had a messed-up family, I'll tell you."

I thought I was going to cry. My behavior in the Gaheimer House had been so cool, so uncaring, and she had been standing in the presence of a person she admired so much.

I suddenly felt the need to get out of there quickly. "Well, thank you for your time, Fern."

Fern didn't want to let me go, now that she had me in her house. "Would you like some tea?"

"No, thank you, I really have to get going. I've got somebody that I need to see."

"You know, I talked to her that morning."

I stopped in my tracks just before the door. Slowly, I turned to face her. "What?" The hair raised on the back of my neck and my eyes watered. "You talked to her on Friday morning? The morning she died?"

"Yes."

"But I thought she didn't call in sick or anything."

"She didn't call the shop, she called me here at my house. I was off that day."

"What time?"

"About nine-thirty. She called to tell me to remember to bring the paperback novels on Saturday. We shared books. I'd buy five or six books a week, and then I'd let her read them, then the next week she'd buy them and let me read them. But she let me keep all of the books. She wouldn't take them."

"Did you notice anything different?"

"No. Things were like they always were. You know, the teakettle was whistling, the dog was yappin'. Life was the same."

We shared a silent moment and then she finally added, "You think if she had known it was her last hours, she would have done anything different?"

I couldn't answer that, so I only shook my head.

"Well, I really must go, Ms. Kennard."

"Fern," she said. "Call me Fern."

"You come to the museum opening, you hear? I'll be looking for you?"

"Okay, I will."

I was thoroughly and completely stunned by the time I made it to my car and was on the highway. Did Sheriff Brooke know that Fern had spoken to Norah that morning? Did it really make any difference to his case? It might narrow down the times more. It could make a difference in somebody's alibi.

•

Rita answered the door almost before I had rung the doorbell. Miss Perfect didn't look the least bit disheveled or upset. I wondered if she slept in complete makeup and ironed clothes.

162

"Torie, I'm glad you came," she said.

I couldn't help but think that she would change her mind by the time I left. I was holding a folder in my left hand, which she kept looking at nervously. I could see behind her facade, and suddenly she didn't seem so perfect to me anymore.

I handed her the folder. "It's Norah's family tree," I said. "There is probably a lot more that could be done on it, but I did five generations back. There are copies of original documents as well. I also wrote a summary for each ancestor, stating their religion, occupation, that sort of thing."

"Oh, thank you so much, Torie. I wish Mom could see it," she said. "Let's go out on the patio for some lemonade."

I followed her onto the patio and she motioned for me to have a seat. The patio furniture most likely cost more than my living-room furniture. The backyard was large and landscaped. Little pebbles and fountains decorated almost every square foot. How odd that there were no yard toys: swing set, sandbox, pool. Rita had small children. Where were their monuments?

"I want to be straight with you, Rita," I said. I watched her place a perfectly poised smile on her face. "I spoke with your father the other day."

"How dare you!" she snapped.

Oooh, a reaction. Why did Rita and Jeff react in the exact same way? Why didn't they want me to speak with their father?

"You have no right—"

I put a hand up to calm her. "He invited me," I explained.

"So what did he tell you?" she asked. She poured the lemonade with a slight tremor in her hands. "That my mother was frigid? That she was obsessed with her father?"

Before I could answer, she was bent down right in my face, just inches away. "He is a bastard!" she yelled, at which point I jumped. With one sentence, she was coming apart at the seams. "He probably also told you that I lost my virginity at thirteen. That I was a drug addict and an alcoholic. That I'd do anything to get my mother's attention. Mom was a selfish woman that couldn't take her eyes off of Jeff. Jeff was her whole world and nobody else existed!" she said. She gulped her lemonade. It was the most unfeminine thing that I had ever seen her do.

"And Jeff. He was to blame, really. If Mom was not totally absorbed in him one hundred percent of the time, he'd go nuts. Temper tantrums, like a two-year-old," she said, waving her arms wildly, pacing back and forth. "Once, he smashed all of the windows on the ground level of our house because Mom wanted to go to the theater instead of his basketball game. Pretty soon she just gave him what he wanted. It was easier. And that's when I ceased to exist."

I hadn't even asked a question yet.

"Actually, he didn't say a word about any of it. He said you were jealous of anything that walked, and that Jeff was obsessive, but he never mentioned virginity, drugs, smashed windows, none of it."

It was ruthless, I know. And I loved every minute of it. I wanted to see her sweat. I wanted to see her dawning realization of the fact she'd just told on herself.

"Instead, he mentioned that he was a pervert and that he wanted Sheriff Brooke's investigation to look elsewhere. He said he didn't kill your mother and that an investigation might bring to light his less than normal sex life."

"Oh my God," she said, sitting down on the patio chair. "The bastard shifted the suspicion to Jeff and me."

"Well, it was done very subtly." I'm sure that didn't make her feel any better, but I didn't know what else to say.

"I can tell you right now," she said, "I didn't kill Mother. I can't stand the sight of blood."

I never wanted to slap somebody so badly in all of my life. She couldn't stand the sight of blood. Not that she loved her mother too much to kill her.

"Besides, I have an alibi. I was at the gym. Twenty people saw me. There's no way Jeff killed her. Number one, he was at the vet, and besides, he was obsessed with her. He adored her. When she said she was going to try and find her father, he went berserk. That'd be more attention given to somebody other than him. He couldn't have done it."

"Then who?" I asked.

"I'd say her father or my father."

"What would make you say her father? Eugene Counts?" Rita was unaware that Eugene was dead and Michael Ortlander had replaced him. I did put it in my report, along with Eugene's real date of death, but she hadn't looked at that yet.

"Jeff told me the other day that Mom had put an ad in the paper, and that her father had answered it. Maybe he had something to hide. All I know is that things were fine until then."

"Why didn't you mention this before?" I asked angrily.

"Because I'd just assumed that she died before she got the chance to meet with him. Now I wonder."

I was in no better shape than I had been before. And I still had no clue as to how to approach the topic of John Murphy. What was it Rita had said earlier? She would do anything to get her mother's attention. Was that it? She'd even go so far as to have an affair with her mother's boyfriend.

Out with the poison, Mom had said. Just do it, get it over with.

I still don't know what kept her from hitting me. And I still have no idea how I got the nerve up, but I straightened my shoulders and just blurted it out. "You were sleeping with John Murphy, weren't you?"

Her first reaction was the one that let me know I had hit home. The reaction that played across her face and her entire body lasted a split second before she had the chance to recover from the shock. It told the truth.

"You bitch!"

"Yes, I'm a bitch, but I'm also right."

Smoldering eyes watched me, trying to feel just how much I knew for sure. Her temples were throbbing from the blood rushing, I could tell. She reached up to rub one of them absentmindedly. "Get the hell off of my property."

"I spoke to Cora Landing. What was she anyway? Did Jeff put her up to propositioning John, to try and get him away from Norah or from you? You wanted to inflict pain on your mother, but you didn't have the guts to go all the way and actually get caught. Cora was there the day you tried to run John Murphy down in your car," I said. I got up and began walking through the yard toward the gate.

"Off my property!"

"I'm going."

"Out!"

"You people make me sick. You made that woman's life a living hell."

"You don't know a damn thing about me and my family."

"I know enough to see that she was used from every angle that was possible by you and everybody else to get what they wanted. You, Jeff, John, Harold. All of you. You should be ashamed of yourselves." I tried to pick up my stride because it suddenly occurred to me that I had insulted the woman on her own property. That's sort of like sawing off the end of the board that you're sitting on. My uncle Melvin did that once. It was a dangerous thing to do.

"You pompous—"

"No, I think not, Mrs. Schmidt. I am not the least bit pompous," I said. "Merely stating the facts. You and your family are the pompous ones. You walk around like you own the world, and you're all a bunch of dysfunctional lunatics."

I got to the gate, finally, and looked back at her. She hugged herself as if it were January; a tear ran down her cheek.

"I noticed that you never did deny it, Rita," I said with as much compassion as I could possibly muster for her.

She simply nodded, I assumed as a confession. "How awful we must seem to you."

Yes. They were quite possibly the most awful people I had ever met. But I remembered what Harold Zumwalt had told me the day I had lunch with him. *Until you've lived in our world, don't be so quick to judge.* I had no idea what I'd be like if I'd been raised in Rita's shoes. By Harold Zumwalt. I'd like to think I'd still be a decent person, but who knows. So I said to her what my father always says to me.

"It doesn't really matter, in the end, what I think. It's what you think of yourselves. After all, you're the only one that has to look at yourself in the mirror."

Just then that damn mad terrier ran from behind the bushes and tried to get out the gate, smearing my bare legs with mud in the process.

"Damn it, Sparky. Get down!" Rita yelled.

One of those weird things happened to me then. It wasn't déjà vu, but something similar in feeling. My brain released some little speck of information from wherever it had stored it. Just a flash, but just enough.

"Rita, when did Sparky get his shots?"

"On Friday."

"Jeff picked him up Thursday?"

"Yeah, and kept him overnight. He'd return him the next day after the visit. Why?"

"No reason."

Twenty

I arrived home, shaken and reeling from information. Some of which I wish I had never heard. Sheriff Colin Brooke's car was out front, and I could just imagine how he must have felt inside my house, with my mother, her ex-husband, and four other musicians.

When I entered my home, Dad raised his eyebrow. That means "Hiya kid" without having to stop picking his guitar. I walked quickly through the living room and into the kitchen, to find it empty. Of course, Mom had to be on the back porch. Where else could she go to get away from the racket?

Mom wore her lavender pantsuit, and Sheriff Brooke wore his usual jeans and T-shirt, and was sitting in a chair opposite Mom.

I could tell the minute I stepped onto the porch that either something was wrong or I'd interrupted something. I must have been wearing the day's events on my face because my mother immediately said to me, "What's wrong?"

"Nothing. Well, all sorts of things, but that's not relevant. What's up?"

"I just came by to tell you," Sheriff Brooke said, "that the plates I ran down belong to a golfing buddy of Ortlander's."

"And what about the car on Norah's street?"

"A pizza delivery."

"Oh. Strikeout."

"Yes," he said.

"I'm going upstairs for a minute," I said, and walked through the kitchen back to the living room.

"Hey, Torie," Uncle Melvin said. "Wanna sing some more?"

"Nah," I said, rounding the banister to head upstairs. "I've had my evening in the spotlight. Enough to last me, oh, at least the next ten years." They all laughed, and as I stepped onto the landing upstairs, I heard one of them say that I was a halfway decent singer. Which is actually a compliment in the highest regards.

I got in the shower and let the hot water run over my head. I stood there immobile for at least ten minutes, just running the events of the last two days through my head.

Jeff had lied about the last time he saw his mother. He said that he saw her last on Thursday when he picked up the dog. But the dog was at Norah's house that morning because Fern had heard it on the phone. Which meant that for some reason he didn't take the dog to the vet for its eleven o'clock appointment, but picked it up later, because the dog was then missing when the police arrived.

No dog Thursday night. Dog Friday morning. No dog Friday afternoon.

Why would he lie? Unless he had no real alibi and got scared and made one up.

Rita was definitely having an affair with John Murphy, who by the way still had no alibi, and I was seriously beginning to doubt his sincerity at being so shook up. An affair, I could forgive him. But with Rita?

And what of the ominous Michael Ortlander? Definitely violent tendencies. He'd committed murder at least four times before, and according to Rita, had actually answered Norah's ad. Something that she probably could have told me, if the damn delivery boy hadn't had incredibly bad timing and come to the door just as I called her that Thursday night.

And of course, the one thing that I was trying to keep completely out of my mind was Sylvia. Why had Hermann Gaheimer left her a million and something dollars? Why had he written, "my beloved Sylvia"? I didn't think anybody had ever referred to Sylvia as "beloved" in her life. "Old battle-ax" seemed much more appropriate. All right, I'll say it. Could they have been . . . lovers?

No. Then why? Hermann had been married, had children for God's sake, and he gave everything to a twenty-something neighbor?

I got out of the shower and picked up the phone and dialed the number that was on the veterinarian's receipt that I still had sitting on my desk.

"Animal Care, Terri speaking."

"Yes, this is . . . Rita Schmidt," I said. "I'm trying to get my mother's accounts straightened out and I was wondering if you could help me with a receipt that I have."

"Who's your mother?"

"Norah Zumwalt. The dog is a terrier named Sparky."

"Oh, hello, Rita. Didn't recognize your voice right away."

"I've got a cold."

"I hate summer colds."

"Yeah, me, too."

"Which day were you concerned with?"

"May the second," I said.

"Oh, I see your confusion," she said. "Jeff called and had the appointment moved to Thursday that week, because he had something to do on Friday. That's why the receipt has the wrong date on it. Did you need anything else?"

Which meant he returned the dog on either Thursday night or early Friday morning. So what happened to it Friday afternoon? It was gone when the police arrived and somehow Rita ended up with it. It was my guess that whoever returned the dog to Rita was the person who killed Norah. Or maybe Rita took the dog with her after killing her mother?

God, that was a terrifying thought. Especially after I'd just confronted her with her affair with John Murphy. On her property no less.

"Hello," Terri asked. "Are you there?"

"Yes," I said. "Thank you."

I hung up the phone and stood in my towel, pondering just

what this could mean. Jeff's sudden lack of an alibi was quite damning.

"Hey, baby," a voice said from behind me.

I screamed and turned around with a jump. It was Rudy.

"Are you undressed for me?"

"God, no," I said. "I mean, I didn't mean it like that. You scared the pee out of me."

"You look like you've seen a ghost," he said.

"I think I just discovered who killed Norah. Based on Rita's answer to one vital question."

He rolled his eyes. "Who is it?"

"Depends on Rita's answer, but it might be Jeff."

"Her own son? Well, I hope you figure it out soon because we'd like to have you back," he said smiling. "By the way, Sheriff Brooke called."

"He did? He was just here a few minutes ago."

"Your mother said he left forty-five minutes ago."

I must have really been zoned out in the shower. I couldn't believe that much time had passed. "What did he want?"

"He said for you to meet him up in Arnold at a place called the Dump. Said he had to show you something that you would find interesting."

"Why there? I mean, that place is a dump, no pun intended," I said. "Besides, didn't it flood?"

"No, I think they sandbagged and they saved it."

"All right. I'll try not to be too late, though. I have the museum opening tomorrow, and I don't have the article finished yet," I said.

After I dressed, I headed downstairs. The first thing I noticed was that it was quiet. I went in the kitchen and found Mom. "Hey, where's Dad and the gang?"

"Crashed out on the back porch."

Taking a peek out the back-door window, I saw Dad lying on the hammock, with Uncle Melvin lying directly under him on the floor. Just how they slept as children. Bob Gussey was asleep in the rocker, one of the chickens pecking at his shoes. Pete Ramey sat sleeping upright in the swing, with Josh Rizzoni curled up on it with his head in Pete's lap. After they slept off the last two days of beer and music, they'd get up and start all over again. When they were young, this was an "artist" thing. Now, I think they were just trying to relive their youth. Which I suppose is fine.

"I'm headed up to Arnold to meet with Sheriff Brooke. I hope I'll be back pretty soon."

"Okay. Rudy's parents are bringing Rachel and Mary home early tomorrow morning on their way to church."

"Good. I really miss them."

"They've only been gone a day."

"No, I mean I've been so wrapped up with Norah's murder and such that I just haven't given them the appropriate attention," I said guiltily. "I think I may have figured it out, though. I think I might know who killed her."

"Who?" she asked.

"Well, it depends on one piece of information. I think it might have been Jeff."

"Oh, God. How horrible. Well, if you're right then that makes up for everything," she said. "Your children will understand that you've done something really important. Maybe not now, but someday they will. And they'll be proud of you."

"Really? Good, I feel better," I said. I kissed her on top of the head. "I'm going. Tell Rudy that there is a chicken loose out there. See if he can get her put in the coop."

Twenty-one

It was late evening by now, and the sun had started to set. I'd half expected that Rudy was wrong and the Dump would actually be closed. It sat right on the Meramec River, and I didn't think it was worth saving. But the river was held at bay about two feet from its doors by sandbags piled like a perfect fortress all around it. I guess if man wants a beer, come hell or high water, he'll get one.

I couldn't imagine what it was the sheriff wanted to show me. Maybe he had something new on Ortlander, but I knew that Ortlander was not the one that killed Norah. It was either Jeff or John, and I didn't really want to call Rita and ask her which one of them had dropped the dog off. I wanted to let Rita cool off from our conversation earlier. I also thought I'd let Sheriff Brooke handle it from here on out. I'd done my best. I had got him his angle that he didn't have, and in the end it had nothing to do with Norah's family tree. I was finished with this.

I threw my purse on my shoulder and entered the Dump, waiting a few seconds to let my eyes focus through the thick fog of cigarette smoke. I glanced around and didn't see Sheriff Brooke. Come to think of it, I hadn't seen his bright yellow car outside either.

When my eyes adjusted, I saw a set of eyes staring at me, as if he were in a trance. It was John Murphy. And he was staring at my pretty little neck as if he were Count Dracula.

I turned to leave the bar. I could only think of one reason that he would be in this bar. He had killed Norah Zumwalt. Before I had the chance to make it to the door, a hand landed on my shoulder. I knew it was John before I even turned around. I breathed deeply, trying to steady my shaking hands, and turned to face him.

"What a coincidence," I said. "I'm meeting Sheriff Brooke here."

"Don't play stupid," he said, cutting my game plan in two. "I made that call to your house."

Funny. If somebody would have asked me two days earlier to describe John Murphy, I would have said that he was a handsome man. Now, he looked twisted and sadistic, nearly ugly.

"Everybody knows where I am. I've also told several people about you. They'll figure it out." I don't suppose I have ever been more terrified in my whole life than I was when he spoke his next sentence.

"I don't care," he said.

It was at that moment that I knew he'd kill me. He was afraid of nothing and had nothing to lose. There was no Achilles' heel that I could find, no crack in his armor.

That made him the most dangerous man alive.

Before I could react, he yanked me by the hair of my head and spun me around the room.

"Help!" I yelled. "I don't know this man!"

To my horror, the men in the bar raised their glasses and cheered in respect for a man that knew how to keep his woman in line.

"Help!" I said. I kept hoping to hit the right frequency that would signal somebody in the bar that this was for real.

"That'll teach her to keep her sweet ass home!" somebody yelled.

My purse beat against my side, reminding me of the letter opener that I'd shoved in it days before. I'd never taken it out. Once in my purse it's in there for life. John pulled me out the door of the bar. I had this perverted notion that I'd actually be better off alone with him than in that bar.

It was warm outside. Muggy. He still had my hair locked in his fingers. We were now headed to his car. I knew if I ever got into it, I'd never get out of it alive. Just look what he'd done to Norah.

I reached into my purse, but the letter opener eluded me. My breathing was constricted from fear, and my hands shook. My right hand closed on an item in my purse, but it wasn't the letter opener. A bottle of something . . . breath freshener.

"Let go of me," I managed. "Please."

We were two feet from his car, John making sounds more animal than human, when he paused to reach for the door. I fumbled with the bottle, flipping the lid off with my thumb. I didn't wait for just the right moment—I wasn't thinking that clearly. I just aimed the container in the direction of his face and hoped that it got in his eyes. I sprayed over and over. Finally, it hit where I wanted it to.

Releasing me instantly, he called me everything he could think of. Finally, I found the letter opener. I tried to run, but he clutched the bottom of my purse, so I just let it slide off my arm. I was running. Freedom felt great. I reached my car. Sickness set in when I realized my keys were in my purse. The purse that hung at the end of John Murphy's hand. I glanced around and ran in the only direction I could: toward the river. I flew over the wall of sandbags and into the water, which reached my knees. I thought I'd run along the riverbank and lose him. Then when it was safe I'd find a street and go for help. There was just one problem. There was no riverbank, due to the flooding. There was muddy, stinking water everywhere.

"Victory!" he yelled from behind.

I stopped, afraid that the sloshing water would give away my location. It was nearly dark. I could see the outline of trees and abandoned buildings along with a few lights through the woods here and there.

My scalp bled from John nearly yanking me bald, and I had this incredible urge to cry. Gripping the letter opener, I looked diligently for a place to hide. All I could find was a house, half-flooded even on stilts. If I could get there without him seeing me, he might give up. Not likely, but I was trying desperately to be optimistic.

Water inched higher up on my body, just below my breasts. Putrid debris floated and clung to the trunks of the trees, tangled in their limbs. Mosquitoes buzzed all around my ears, and I resisted swatting at them for fear that John would hear me.

The ground was gone now. I had to swim. Finally, the house was before me, and I was on the bottom floor, which had two feet of water standing on it. Rotted furniture was strewn in no particular order. I felt something slither past my leg and I found myself less afraid of the snake than I was of John Murphy, and considered that a good sign.

"Mrs. O'Shea, I know you're here."

He was right outside the house and coming in. I found the staircase and ran up it. The wood was rotted and my foot slipped down between the decayed planks. I winced in pain, knowing I'd been cut from it, gave a momentary thought to everything I could contract from that exposed flesh, and went on up the stairs.

When I reached the second floor, I realized that I had trapped myself.

"Why didn't you leave it alone? After I'd warned you," he said. "She didn't deserve to live. She was weak."

I could hear him as he found the stairs, and I knew that I had nowhere to hide. He'd find me in a closet, as I knew from experience, so I stood in the middle of the room and waited for him. It was dark, and only a vague outline of anything was visible.

"The woman never stood up to anything in her life. Never. She let her children walk all over her. She wouldn't marry me. She was always the diplomat." He came into view just then, what I could make of him.

"You killed her for that?" I asked. I thought if I asked him enough questions, I'd buy some time. For what I didn't know. A rescue? My heart pounded over and over—I could feel it in my throat. I was dizzy, either from the bleeding on my scalp, or from the rush of blood from my heart pounding.

"She changed. Who would have guessed that she would grow a backbone?" he said. "I thought if I screwed her little girl enough times that I'd get a reaction from her. I'd force her to make a decision."

"Only you didn't bargain for the decision she gave you."

"She became enraged. Said she was going to leave me for good."

"So if you couldn't have her nobody else could either?"

"Yes. I'd spent years with that woman. I suffered through those wacked-out children of hers, all her hang-ups, and in the end . . . she was going to dump me."

He was holding something in his right hand. It was a good ten inches long, and I assumed that it was a knife. I knew that my letter opener was greatly inferior.

"Wait a minute," I said. "This wasn't about love or adoration. This was about money. You can pretend that it was some higher reason, but it was just the money. You thought eventually she'd marry you, and then you'd have her money. Or you'd kill her then and inherit the money."

"Very good, Mrs. O'Shea," he said.

"What about the dog? Are you the one that gave Rita the dog?"

He took a few steps closer to me, and I stiffened instinctively.

"That dog was carrying on like it was rabid. All I could think to do with it was take it with me," he said, "just so it would shut up. I didn't need the neighborhood alerted. I mean, I hadn't actually intended to kill her. I just got so angry."

"I don't believe that for a minute."

He came at me with a force full of hatred and vengeance. I stepped back and screamed. I gripped the letter opener. My palms sweated so badly that I nearly dropped it. I raised the opener as high as I could, shaking all the while. I shoved it into his shoulder. It shocked him more than it hurt him, but it bought me a precious few seconds. I went for the window, realizing that the water would break my fall. Why hadn't I thought of that before?

I heard a whish by my ear. It was his knife. He missed and I stepped farther away from him. He lunged for me, and grabbed my hurt ankle. It stung more than it actually hurt. The force of him falling to the floor was more than the rotted wood could take. It split and we fell to the first floor with such force, it took my breath away for a few seconds, the water stinging my back.

Each of us was splashing, trying to be the first to stand. I still hadn't gotten my breathing back to normal from the fall, and I felt fairly ragged. He grabbed me from behind, and I rolled to my back and saw the letter opener still lodged in his shoulder. I broke a foot free and kicked it, sending new pain racing through him.

This time, he punched me in the face, and I cried out in pain. The room spun. I felt a tooth pop and tasted blood, mixed with disgusting river water. He must have lost his knife somewhere in the fall, because he was intent upon drowning me. And he would have succeeded.

I tried to get to my feet to get away from him. He pushed me down into the water, his hands around my throat. I fought him with every ounce of energy I could muster. My feet kicked, my hands were on his face. I dug what fingernails I had into his face, hoping to hit an eye.

I pushed up with my stomach muscles, my body shaking from the strain. It was enough to get my face out of the water, but I still couldn't get a breath. I had shifted positions enough that I could bring my knee up. I shoved it into his groin as hard as I could. His hands came loose, and I breathed too soon, sucking in river water.

I choked and sputtered on the water caught in my windpipe. I was sitting up now. There was no way that I could fight a grown man and win, and I knew it. Instinctively I scooted away from him. I felt a board crack beneath me. When he lunged this time, I leaned back on the board. It popped from my weight, the end of it shooting up out of the water. And right into the stomach of John Murphy.

NEW KASSEL GAZETTE

✍

THE NEWS YOU MIGHT MISS
by Eleanore Murdoch

Tobias Thorley wants everybody to know that he takes his garden seriously. Now his statue of General Custer is missing. He plans to install motion detectors. This is a warning.

The New Kassel Bowlers did terribly poorly this year in the regional tournament. We will not even say where they placed. Bowlers are needed! Please sign up to replace the ones we have.

Also, the most exciting piece of news . . . Torie O'Shea has become our resident Terminator. She not only solved the murder of Norah Zumwalt, but actually fought the murderer and lost a tooth! It's like the movies!

Good news. The floodwater has receded by two feet. It is going down! Let's hope that it doesn't deter the people from attending the opening of our new museum, which has already been put off a week.

Until next time. Torie, I await anxiously your next adventure.

Eleanore

Twenty-two

Somewhere, an accordion played.

It was the opening of the museum, which had been put off a week so that I could recuperate.

I stood in the New Kassel Museum, which was a two-hundred-year-old cabin relocated on the Gaheimer House grounds. I was in a re-created gown of 1889. It was a purple paisley gown with a slim skirt and smocking. It had a high neck, with wide lapels and slightly puffed sleeves. I even had an open lace parasol and large hat that Carmen Miranda would have died for except it was topped with flowers and feathers instead of fruit.

I had finished the flood display, complete with photographs of then and now. Wilma thought it was in dreadful taste, but Sylvia thought it most enlightening.

Sylvia stood next to me as I watched the first of the patrons file through the front door. I had said nothing to her about my discovery of Gaheimer's will, and so far she hadn't asked.

"Did you get all the information from the newspaper filing cabinet?" she asked.

"Yes," I said.

"Did you happen to look in the other filing cabinet on the opposite side of the room?" she asked. Her eyes narrowed. She wore a huckleberry silk dress, and pearl earrings. She looked quite lovely. Except for the suspicious look on her face.

"If I did, Sylvia, I would never tell anybody anything that I had seen."

She blushed. "Did I say that I was worried about that? I simply want to know if you were snooping where you weren't supposed to be."

She was determined to make me give her a straight answer. "Yes. I looked."

"And what did you see?" she asked me.

"Nothing of importance."

"You've ruined everything, you know." She didn't look at me now; she looked around the room. "Hermann did not want me to be scarred by the scandal. I can't expect you to understand," she said finally.

"I understand that you were very young and in love. I don't think Mr. Gaheimer was as worried as you think. He would not have written his will with such affection."

"What do you mean?" she asked.

" 'My beloved Sylvia,' " I said. "I think you were the one more concerned with what people would think. It's okay, Sylvia. I won't tell a soul. And for what it's worth, I don't condemn you in the least." In fact, it had actually shown me that Sylvia had been human. She had felt the most human of all emotions.

"You can't possibly know," was all she said. Evidently there was much more to it than I knew, or would ever know.

Just then Sheriff Brooke came in the building with my mother, my husband, and my daughters. I was relieved that nobody had been hurt in this adventure. All of my family and friends were safe. John Murphy, however, was very much dead.

I had listened to the sheriff give me a forty-minute lecture on the dangers of crime fighting. If I didn't know better, I would swear that he was reading off of cue cards written by my mother and Rudy. He was right, of course. But I had also caught a murderer. I felt . . . well, I'm not sure how I felt.

The state was building a case against Michael Ortlander, at this moment, for the murders of Gwen Geise, Stella McClellan, Dorothy Davis, and the real Eugene Counts. It was quite possible that due to the age of these cases, he would never even go to trial. The case was old, and the trail cold. And I was going to have to appear in court to testify as to how I figured out his true identity. If this went to court, I would be needing the advice of my friend Colette more than ever.

I took great pride in telling Louise Shenk that her brother had not abandoned them. I wasn't very thrilled to tell her that he'd been murdered by his friend. But the knowledge that he had not betrayed them made up for it. John Murphy had actually gone through with signing over the insurance money to Louise, I'm sure in an effort to proclaim his innocence all the more. Part of the money that she received was going to move Eugene Counts's body to rest next to his mother, and for the first time in fifty years, put his correct name on the tombstone. When I visited her she cried, and was able to truly mourn her brother.

I had received a call from the Hill Top Nursing Home in yet another twist to this tale. Florence Ortlander had died in her sleep, at peace. The shocking thing was that she had left me that beautiful mauve Lone Star quilt that she had made. It now graces my bed, as it should, in a home full of love. I said a silent thank-you to God that I didn't have to face her. She would have been able to read my face, and I just couldn't destroy the fantasy of her only son.

My father walked in the door behind the rest of my family, looked around the room, and smiled at me. They all descended on me at the same time.

"Mom, you look so pretty," Rachel said.

"Well, thank you."

Dad came up next to me and hit me on the chin as he usually does, only this time, it hurt, thanks to the molar that I lost in the struggle with John Murphy.

"So," he said. "Haven't talked to you in a while. What's new?"

Rudy laughed and slapped him on the shoulder. "You need to come out of your shell a little more, Pop."

Mary tried to hug my leg through all of the skirts and undergarments. I hugged her back as best as I could.

"Sheriff," I said. "Have you spoken to Rita?"

"Yes," he said.

"What did she say?" I asked. I had been wondering why she had not said anything about seeing John Murphy on Friday when he had dropped off Sparky.

"She said that it never occurred to her that anything was suspicious because John did take the dog to the groomers and to the vet once in a while, if Jeff was busy. It wasn't until much later, when she realized that John was supposed to be out of town from Thursday night through the whole weekend, that she realized something wasn't right. She mentioned it to her brother Jeff and never gave it any more thought," he said. "I believe her. It never occurred to her that John would be capable of murder. So she just dismissed it."

It would be a horrible thing to know that you'd been sleeping with a man capable of murder. Capable of murdering your mother. Maybe that would be punishment enough for her sins.

Jeff, on the other hand, had not dismissed it. He confronted John Murphy with the discrepancy in time. John passed him some lie, but he knew if Jeff could figure out the discrepancy it would only be a matter of time until I did. Which was why he came after me when he did. Jeff had actually called to thank me for everything and even called his newfound aunt Louise to see if she needed anything. I suppose people can change.

"Victory," my mother said. "Sheriff Brooke has exciting news."

"Really?" I asked. I looked from her to him. "What is it?"

"I bought Norah's antique shop," the sheriff said.

"You're kidding?"

"No, really."

"Are you hanging up your badge?" I asked.

"No. I just always wanted to own an antique shop. Besides, I like this town. I think I'm going to keep the name, though."

Norah's Antiques. Poor Norah.

Her life had not been her own. It was a nightmare from day one. Jeff insisted that his mother had spoken to Michael Ortlander, under the illusion that he was Eugene Counts. I couldn't help but wonder if she had taken one look at him and known the truth.

She led a very sad life. Controlled by her husband, her children, and in a way, by the father she never knew. I was reminded of the words of one of my favorite authors, Henry James: "Three things in human life are important. The first is to be kind. The second is to be kind. And the third is to be kind."

If only somebody had shown some kindness to her.

Sheriff Brooke leaned close to my ear then, and whispered, "Now I can be closer to your mother."